REM

WAR
Copyright © REMINGTON KANE, 2015
YEAR ZERO PUBLISHING

CHAPTER 1 - It begins!

12:14 a.m.

Tanner lay on his stomach atop a Midtown Manhattan roof, and sighted in on the back of Sara Blake's head.

He was over half a mile away from Sara's apartment and peering through the riflescope of a Barrett 98B sniper rifle, while he lay concealed from sight beneath the base of a large pigeon coop.

It was one of three shooting positions that he had scouted out in the days since his return to New York City, and he had made careful plans for both his assassination of Sara Blake, and his escape from the scene, whether he be successful or not.

He had underestimated the woman once and it almost cost him his life, he would not make that mistake again, and was prepared.

Sara was seated on the sofa inside her living room with the drapes drawn shut. However, Tanner had taken note that whenever the central air system cycled on, it did so with an exuberant rush of air, which stirred the drapes and caused them to separate as much as a quarter inch, a quarter inch gap that happened to line up with Sara's accustomed position on her sofa.

Tanner had been lying inside the shooting blind for over five hours. He was hot; he was sweaty, thirsty, and quite sick of smelling bird shit.

Still, he was waiting for the perfect shot, for that ideal confluence of events when Sara would be seated in the right spot, at the exact moment the central air kicked on, and when the gap between the drapes was at its widest, to allow viewing.

And one more factor needed to be present—confirmation. He wanted to see her profile at the very least, to confirm that he was killing the right woman.

Through the scope, Tanner saw the flutter of the drapes as a gap appeared, through which he could spy Sara's skull, the dark hair luminescent beneath the ceiling lights inside her apartment.

The head turned just as the gap was closing, and Tanner saw the left side of her face.

He fired, and the .338 Lapua Magnum Cartridge round left the barrel of the rifle at more than double the speed of sound and entered Sara's apartment.

However, the window didn't shatter, despite the wispy spider web of cracks that emanated outward from where the supersonic round entered.

Tanner sighed.

This was one tough woman to kill.

He knew from the failure of the window to shatter, that it must be made of ballistic glass, and given that, it also meant that the view seen through the material was likely altered to be a distorted one.

Sara Blake wasn't sitting where she had appeared to be, but rather, up to a foot to the right or the left.

Tanner smiled grudgingly.

The woman was good.

The drapes on the apartment window flew open and, in the light of a setting sun, Tanner saw a man wearing a bulletproof vest place an instrument to the glass directly over the hole his round had made.

He then saw the red beam of a laser and knew that the device was designed to pinpoint where the shot had originated.

Tanner sighed again.

It was time to move.

He crawled out from under the pigeon coop and used the scope on the rifle to look across at Sara's building. The man with the laser tracker, an older man with a crooked nose, was speaking into a two-way radio and undoubtedly relaying Tanner's position to troops in the area.

They would come and take over the building as they attempted to hunt him down. That meant that the guard in the lobby would be knocked out, killed, or detained, and that Tanner would have to leave by the alley exit.

That was fine, because he had planned for such a contingency.

How many and of what breed were the troops, Tanner didn't know, but he had decided ahead of time to use non-lethal force to aid in his escape.

The men coming for him could be paid mercenaries, but might as easily be cops or Feds. In any event, they were coming, and from what Tanner now knew of Sara Blake, he expected the woman to send an army after him.

Let them come, Tanner thought. He was ready.

Tanner was dressed in lightweight body armor and carried two Glocks with magazines packed with rubber bullets.

The bullets were ones that he had fashioned himself, and each round held two spheres of hard rubber. The rounds would sting, and at their worst, break a bone, but anyone struck by them should live.

Tanner had no desire to kill a cop, and if his adversaries were mercenaries instead, he also didn't want to kill them and give birth to an official investigation.

His goal was to escape, so that he could make another attempt at Sara, who was the true threat to him, and who he was impressed by, despite the risk she represented.

Tanner entered the stairway that led down from the roof and paused to secure the helmet on his head. It too was armored, although a round of any significance would pierce it with scant difficulty.

Over the body armor, Tanner wore a harness, such as the type used by mountain climbers, and as he headed down the stairs with a gun held in his right hand, there was a length of climbing rope draped over one shoulder, and he also wore a tactical belt that had large pouches located at its sides.

Tanner proceeded down while moving swiftly, but paused at every other landing to listen.

When he was on the 17th floor of the 40-story building he heard the sound of footsteps slapping against the concrete stairs as what sounded like a dozen men came running up the steps.

Tanner peeked over the railing and saw that his count had been off. There were sixteen of them, all armed, and they were advancing in four groups of four, while leaving a gap of half a flight of stairs between them.

As they drew closer, Tanner saw that there were no insignias on their clothes, and only a few bulletproof vests, and surmised that they were mercenaries.

That meant that Sara hadn't gone to the authorities, and Tanner knew then that she wanted him dead, not captured, and if captured, he would be tortured.

The sound of running feet came from above as well, as more men entered the stairwell from an upper floor after riding the elevator to the top, and from the sound of them, their force was as great as the men advancing from below.

Tanner smiled. It seemed that Sara wasn't underestimating him either.

When he was ready, Tanner removed an item from a side pants pocket.

It was a remote control detonator.

As both groups of men closed in on his position, Tanner flipped down and activated the night vision optics attached to the helmet, pressed down on a button, and inside the electrical control box that operated the building's lights, a small charge went off, destroying the circuit breakers and plunging the entire building into darkness.

***

Inside her apartment, Sara cursed as she watched the lights go out in a building three blocks away.

"He was prepared."

A man walked over to stand beside her. His name was Duke, he had a beefy build, salt & pepper hair cropped short, and a nose made crooked by virtue of having been broken many times.

"They'll get him, Sara. He's walked into the trap, literally taken his best shot, and now it's our turn. I've got three dozen trained men over there all loaded for bear. Tanner doesn't stand a chance."

The short bark of a laugh came from the sofa, where Johnny Rossetti was drinking a beer.

Duke turned and stared at him.

"Is something funny, Rossetti?"

"Not really, it's just that Tanner has escaped certain death so many times that I would never count him out, and I've already learned the hard way not to attack him."

Sara walked over and stood before Johnny.

"You've just given up? Is that why you wouldn't add your men to Duke's?"

Johnny reached out and took her hand.

"Of course I haven't given up, but I know Tanner now, I thought he was Romeo, but I still know the man, and I'm hoping to find a peaceful solution to this."

Sara ripped her hand away.

"There won't be peace until he's dead."

Johnny sighed.

"Baby, if you don't make peace with this man he'll kill you, and I think you know that."

This time it was Duke's turn to laugh.

"My men have Tanner trapped inside that building. The only way he's coming out of there is feet first."

Johnny shrugged.

"I sent my best men against him and he went through them like a hot knife through butter, including Lars Gruber. You don't beat Tanner; you survive him. The man has no weaknesses."

Johnny's words stirred something in Sara, and she sat beside him on the sofa.

"Didn't you say that Joe Pullo and Tanner were friends?"

"More like friendly, but what's your point?"

"What you said was wrong, Tanner must have a weakness, everyone does. Where is Pullo, I want to speak to him?"

"Joe's busy tonight, but I'm expecting him to call soon, you can talk to him then."

"Alright, and maybe it won't matter. Like Duke said, his mercenaries have Tanner trapped."

Johnny nodded, but if he had to place a bet, his money would be on Tanner.

***

Inside the stairwell, Duke's mercenaries were temporarily confused by the sudden darkness, and while there were emergency lights, Tanner had disabled most of them ahead of time.

However, their confusion changed to shock and fear as Tanner opened fire on them.

His guns were not only silenced but also had inhibitors to reduce the muzzle flash of the weapons, and so they had no idea where the shots were coming from.

Tanner pushed through the four groups as his shots caused chaos, and was past the sixteen startled men before someone had the sense to turn on a flashlight.

The men were so rattled that Tanner heard them fire on their compatriots, who were converging on them from the upper floors.

"Goddamn it, don't fire, it's us," said a male voice.

Another deep voice answered the first.

"Where's Tanner?"

"You didn't get him?"

"No. Shit, he got by us."

When both sets of men were two flights behind him, Tanner leaned down and secured a hook to one of the gray iron balusters set in the stairway railing.

The hook was attached to the rope he carried, and he prepared to lower himself over the side and to make his way down to the bottom, by using the narrow space between the stair banisters.

It would be much faster than walking, and would leave the crowd on the stairs far behind.

Tanner went over the railing, while being careful to keep his legs straight and his toes pointed downward. The gap of space between the flights of steps was little more than a foot wide, and if he wasn't careful, he could injure himself on their metal railings.

He had traveled ten floors when the beam from a flashlight found him and someone jerked the rope.

Tanner's back slammed into the angled edge of the concrete steps and the pain made him gasp. He ignored it, kicked off a railing and dropped atop the opposite set of stairs, just as the men above began firing.

Bullets ricocheted wildly throughout the stairwell, but only a few made it as far as the floor he was on, the fifth floor, without hitting something on the way down and being deflected harmlessly.

Tanner waited it out by keeping his head down, and only one round hit him on the side of the vest, but lacked force because it was a ricochet that had pinged off the railing.

When the shooting ceased, the sound of boots on stairs resumed, as the persistent and single-minded group came barreling down the steps in pursuit.

Tanner stood and extracted two objects from the pouches on the tactical belt he wore. The objects looked like giant firecrackers, but were black and had no fuse. However, they did have a timer, and after pausing to take a guess on just how soon his pursuers would reach his position, he set the timer on one of the objects and tossed it into a corner of the landing above him. The second object he left on the landing of the floor below, and timed it to go off seven seconds after the first one.

The objects were homemade bombs, packed with nails, but were non-lethal, in that the nails they were stuffed with were only a quarter of an inch long, and the chemical-based charge had been calculated to penetrate, but not deeply embed the objects. Still, anyone in their path upon detonation would wish they were anywhere else.

Tanner's decision not to kill the men didn't mean that he had no intention of not hurting them. They needed to know that there was a price for hunting him, and a price usually paid in death would be paid for in pain instead.

Tanner headed downward as the men neared the twin charges, and was on the second floor landing when the first blast went off, and from the sound of the screams, his timing had been perfect.

The first blast caught the men at the rear of the posse as they rounded the staircase and shredded the backs of their legs, causing the men to fall down and collide into their comrades in front of them.

One man suffered a broken kneecap, another a broken leg, and three more broke either an arm or a wrist, while the men unlucky enough to be the recipients of the nails each had dozens of puncture wounds in their legs, backs, and buttocks.

"Move, move, move!" one of the men shouted, fearful, and rightfully so, about a second charge going off.

Only two of the men attempted to help their wounded comrades, and they would be rewarded for their good deed by being the only two left unscathed, while the rest of their fellows fled down the stairs, just in time to greet the second blast.

More bones were broken, more legs cut and embedded by nails, and one particularly unlucky man lost an eye, but all the men on the stairs shared one trait, they had learned the folly of attacking a man like Tanner. They were also aware that Tanner had chosen to spare them, and that the blasts could have been lethal.

Still, they were hired to do a job and, after recovering enough to speak, one of the men who had been leading a team reached a bloody hand into a pocket and took out his radio, to send a warning to the team stationed outside, while praying he wasn't too late.

They had knocked out the security guard and chained the lobby doors, but left four men at the alley exit, and those four men needed to be warned that Tanner was headed their way.

"Team Golf, be advised, teams Alpha, Bravo, Charlie, Delta, Echo, and Foxtrot are down. I repeat, we are down, but subject is active and heading your way. Come in."

There were a few seconds of static, and then a voice spoke.

It was Tanner.

"Teams Alpha, Bravo, Charlie, Delta, Echo, and Foxtrot, be advised, team Golf is unconscious and bleeding. Whoever you are, if you come at me again… I'll kill you all."

The radio went dead as Tanner smashed it against the wall, and let the broken pieces fall atop the men he had just shot repeatedly with rubber bullets.

They had been waiting for him outside in the alleyway, after having correctly guessed the path he would use to make his departure from the building.

Tanner had aided them in coming to that assumption by leaving obvious signs that the door lock had been tampered with, leading them to assume that he had entered the building that way, and would be leaving by the same door.

In actuality, Tanner had entered through the front door with a phony ID that identified him as the tenant of an office on the 37th floor. If he had been trapped inside, he wanted to have a reason for being there, and most cops would have just taken the ID at face value and let him walk.

He had performed many difficult hits over the years, and had also escaped many traps because he was meticulous in his preparation.

The ordinance-proof glass at Sara's apartment had been a surprise, but not completely unexpected, and could have been counterbalanced by using an incendiary round that would have set her apartment ablaze.

Tanner had decided against using one, because he couldn't be certain of who else would be in the apartment with her, nor if the blaze would spread to engulf and harm her neighbors.

He was a professional killer, not a mindless butcher, and he was confident that in time he would kill Sara Blake, although, he had to admit, the woman was gifted at surviving.

The men in the alley had been waiting for Tanner to emerge, and were ready to blast him as soon as he stepped out the door. Unfortunately for them, Tanner had placed a cheap cell phone behind the dumpster at their backs before entering the building, and called it a second before making his exit.

Team Golf were all turned towards the dumpster after the phone went off with a shrill ring, and Tanner shot them from behind with the rubber bullets, which, while generally non-lethal, were still devastatingly painful, especially when fired at close quarters.

With the threats handled, Tanner headed for the side street, which was empty of anything other than the occasional passing car.

But, as he stepped from the alleyway after removing his helmet, he nearly shot the man waiting there in the face.

The man was holding his hands up at shoulder level, to reveal that they held no weapons.

"I come in peace."

Tanner sent Joe Pullo a smirk.

"Since when?"

Pullo smiled, and gestured back at the building.

"Are they all dead?"

"They're alive, but they'll remember this night."

"You thought they might be cops, huh?"

"I couldn't be sure, now tell me, why are you here?"

Pullo turned and walked towards his vehicle, a black Hummer.

"We'll take my ride."

Tanner nodded, and off they went to talk.

CHAPTER 2 - The curse of the human race

As they rode along in the Hummer, Tanner asked Joe Pullo a question.

"How did you find me? I know you weren't connected to those Mercs back there."

"Sara Blake sent them after you, but when I saw that building go dark, I knew for sure that was where you were, and I was also following them."

"What do you know about Sara Blake?"

"I know that she wants you dead, and, I also know that she's Johnny's girl."

"Rossetti and Blake are together?"

"Yeah,"

"That's not good. I was hoping to mend things between myself and the Giacconi Family, and once I kill his woman, Rossetti is not likely to want to make friends with me."

Pullo laughed.

"You can say that again, but Johnny already likes you, well actually, he likes Romeo."

"I see that Blake has been talking."

"Oh yeah,"

"It's her or me, Joe. The woman wants me dead and she won't stop coming."

"So I hear, and to tell you the truth, I'm amazed that she's still alive."

"Don't underestimate her. I made that mistake and caught a bullet for it."

"Maybe there's a way to make peace, and that's why I'm here. Are you willing to listen?"

"Yeah, but let's talk over coffee."

***

Inside Sara's apartment, Duke lowered his phone and spoke through gritted teeth.

"The bastard escaped, and he injured most of the men I sent after him while doing it."

Sara took a deep breath before asking a question.

"How many are dead?"

"None, but one man will lose an eye."

Johnny stood and took Sara in his arms. The two of them had grown much closer since her return from Ridge Creek, as she had essentially been a prisoner in her own home as she waited for Tanner to strike.

Her life had been put on hold, and she had even resigned from being an active participant in the financial blog and newspaper, *Street View*, of which she was a part owner.

In truth, her heart had never really been in the financial news business, since she had only acquired *Street View* as a means to an end, at a time when she thought Tanner was dead, and her main target of revenge was the former head of The Conglomerate, Frank Richards.

In a greater sense, Sara's life had been on hold since she found her lover, Brian Ames, murdered, and since that day, all her energies had been directed at exacting revenge on the men who had killed him, and on Tanner in particular.

When Tanner disappeared from sight after their encounter in Pennsylvania, Sara entered a limbo between fear and relief as she waited to learn if Tanner was dead or alive, and if dead, would his body ever be found?

The days of waiting had been unnerving for Sara. Still, she did what she could to prepare for an eventual attack, and tonight those precautions paid off.

During that time of waiting, she and Johnny lived together, as he was unwilling to leave her side for very long, and the two of them had become more than just lovers.

Johnny brushed a stray hair away from Sara's face and caressed her check.

"Okay, we tried Duke's way, now we try mine."

Sara looked up into his face, searching his eyes.

"You have a plan?"

"I do. My plan is to keep you alive."

Duke made a sound of derision.

"Would you care to share some details, or do you just hope that Tanner will go away?"

"I'm going to talk to the man. I know him, somewhat, and I think I can get him to listen."

"How will you get in contact with him?" Sara asked.

"Joe Pullo is working on that right now, but no matter what, baby, I won't let anything happen to you."

Duke placed a suit jacket on over the vest he wore.

"I have to go clean up one hell of a mess. Sara, stay safe honey, and I'll call you tomorrow."

Duke left the apartment and Johnny and Sara settled on a loveseat.

"I'm staying again tonight," Johnny said. "I don't want to leave your side until we know the threat is over."

Sara leaned against him as he wrapped an arm around her.

"I'll only be safe when Tanner is dead."

Johnny said nothing, and hoped that Pullo was able to put his plan in motion.

***

Tanner shed the body armor and tactical belt, and followed Pullo inside an all-night eatery on Sixth Avenue. After inhaling the aroma of the food, both men decided to eat as well, and were enjoying steak and eggs with their coffee while they talked.

"Johnny wants a meet, you, him, and Blake."

"When and where?"

"At the club, tomorrow at nine a.m.,"

Tanner stared at Pullo.

"Rossetti must think I'm stupid. He's asking me to pinpoint my whereabouts for Blake."

"This isn't a trap. You have my word on that, and while I'm talking to you, Johnny will be talking to Blake."

"So, she hasn't agreed to this either?"

"No, and he's not going to tell her until it's time for you to show, that way, she can't plan any double-crosses."

"Rossetti is willing to take my word that I won't kill her?"

"No, but I'll take your word, and he'll take mine, so, what's it going to be, are you willing to talk?"

Tanner said nothing for a moment, but then nodded.

"I'll show. I actually don't want to kill the woman if I don't have to, but I'll tell you right now, I'll have to. She's obsessed with killing me, no, more than that, she wants to torture me, and I don't think there's a damn thing in this world she wants more."

"Because you killed her lover?"

"Yes, he was acting as a rat, giving up info on The Conglomerate, and Richards put out a contract on him."

Pullo smirked.

"The funny thing is, The Conglomerate is dead, at least here it is, we're back to being independent, but the European branch is still hanging on. A German guy named Heinz, Bruno Heinz, has taken Richards' place, and he's as big a bastard as Richards ever was."

"What makes him a bastard?"

"He wants us back in The Conglomerate and won't take no for an answer. He even had Sullivan Silva from Chicago whacked, and then moved one of his people into his slot, also, he owns the MegaZenith building after his company acquired Richards' holdings."

"Does he have people here?"

"That's the rumor, but if they're here, they're lying low."

"You think there will be a war?"

"Maybe,"

Tanner smiled.

"Good, then it sounds like Rossetti can use me, and it's time I got back to work."

"So I can tell him yes, that you'll show at the club tomorrow?"

"Yeah, I'll be there."

"And you won't kill Blake? I have to have your word on that."

"I won't kill her, at least, not until after we've had this meeting."

"Good, then tomorrow at nine it is."

The two men grew silent as they finished eating their meals, but after taking his last bite and wiping his mouth with a napkin, Tanner leaned back in his chair and stared at Pullo.

"How's Laurel doing?"

A flash of surprise crossed Pullo's face, but then his lips curled in a smile.

"I should have figured that you'd know about us."

"Have you told her that I'm alive?"

"Yes, I told her… it seemed to please her."

Tanner nodded, and grew silent.

Pullo pushed his plate aside and leaned forward.

"Do you want her, Tanner? Are you going after Laurel?"

"No, Joe, she's much better off with you. Deep down, Laurel wants the straight life, a home, maybe even a kid, and while you're not a nine-to-five type of guy, you still lead a stable life compared to mine. Plus, I'll never marry, but you would, wouldn't you?"

"Yeah, I'd marry Laurel, someday, if she'd have me."

"Take care of her and I'll keep my distance."

"She loves you, you know that?"

"I know."

"And you?"

Tanner laughed.

"What's so funny?"

"Love, it's the curse of the human race, and makes every man a fool."

"But not you?"

Tanner sighed.

"Not yet,"

CHAPTER 3 - The other Ms. Blake

In the bedroom of her Manhattan apartment, Sara's sister, Jennifer, sighed with contentment as she snuggled deeper into Jake Garner's arms.

The two began dating only a short while ago, after Jennifer saw the news story about Garner's partner, Michelle Geary, being killed in the line of duty.

Garner had been shaken by his partner's sudden death, which took place in front of him, and the emotional comfort that Jennifer offered him in the aftermath soon turned to something more.

Jennifer felt guilty at first and fought her feelings, because she thought that her sister might have eyes for Garner, but, after learning that Sara was with Johnny Rossetti, she gave in to her feelings and took Jake to bed.

It was not a decision she regretted, but often wondered if she would.

"Jake?"

Garner kissed her shoulder.

"Yes?"

"Are you sleeping with someone else?"

"What? No, why would you ask that?"

"Sara, she told me about your reputation. Was she exaggerating?"

Garner released her and sat up on the side of the bed, and Jennifer moved behind him while standing on her knees.

"Jennifer, you're the first woman I've been with since your sister shot me. I nearly died from my wounds, and I had a lot of time to think while I was in the hospital.

Sara didn't exaggerate; I was living like a playboy, but… I want more now."

"And you wanted to be with Sara, didn't you?"

Garner turned his head and looked at her.

"I was attracted to your sister, yes, but there was something else there too. I pity her in a way, because I can understand how much she's suffered for the loss of her lover, I understand that pain only too well."

Jennifer pulled back on Jake's shoulders and bid him to lay down beside her again. He did so, and they lay facing each other.

The bedroom was on the twenty-second floor and was lit only by the glow of the city's lights, casting much of Garner's face in shadow, but even so, Jennifer saw the pain in his eyes.

"You lost someone special once, didn't you?"

"Three people, my wife… and my two children, my boy and my girl."

"Oh my God, what happened?"

"My wife, Wendy, we were children when we married, only eighteen, and she was pregnant with my son. Our age didn't hinder us as it has some young couples. We were so in love that nothing else mattered. We both came from great homes, had supportive parents, and while Wendy raised the baby, I worked six days a week in her father's factory while going to school at night."

Garner paused, as thoughts of the past flooded his mind, and Jennifer saw a smile play at his lips.

"Those were good days, weren't they?" she asked.

"They were the best, even though we had almost no money and lived with my parents. But, the days were full, we were happy, and we had plans, you know? We had our future mapped out, and thanks to our parents helping us, we were able to buy a house by the time our daughter was born."

"You must have still been quite young, no?"

"I was just twenty-two, had a wife and two kids and was entering law school. Life was good, full of family, friends, school, and work. God, what I wouldn't give to go back there for just one more day."

They grew silent for nearly a minute, and then Jennifer asked a question in a voice that was barely a whisper.

"What happened to your family, Jake?"

Garner cleared his throat, and when he spoke, his voice was tight with emotion.

"Ah, our house, our house was new, a tiny place, but new, and the land developer cleared away trees and built more homes above ours after we'd been living there a year. Those homes had great views, were three times the size of ours, but the land they had been built atop… they never should have been built there."

Jennifer held her breath, as she began to suspect what was coming.

"I went out to get ice-cream one night, just a quick trip to the store. It had rained hard for a week, the ground had grown soft, there was a mudslide, and the homes above ours, they, they, fifteen minutes, I was only gone for fifteen minutes, and when I returned, I found my home destroyed, and my family crushed to death… the house above ours. It looked like someone had picked it up and dropped it on my home, and they were gone, all dead."

Jennifer hugged him and felt warm tears wet her shoulder, as Jake sobbed against her. After a few minutes, he regained his composure and spoke.

"I was filled with hate for the developer and the builder. They were brothers, and after that night, they both lost their businesses, the courts awarded me and the other survivors damages which bankrupted them, but I didn't want their money, I wanted their lives."

"You, you didn't…?"

"No, I thought about it constantly, even while I dreamed of becoming an FBI agent, but a year after my family died, one of the brothers committed suicide, while the other died in a drunken bar fight. Still, I understand what your sister is feeling, and I can sympathize with wanting revenge, but in the end, it's yourself that's murdered, and not the one that wronged you."

"And all the women that came after, that was your way of not getting close to anyone, wasn't it?"

"Yes, and I was also using sex to kill the pain, but, after the shooting, I knew I wanted more. I can't have what I lost, but I can sure as hell have more than what I've got, and I can start fresh, make a new life."

Jennifer kissed him.

"Am I a part of that new life?"

Garner smiled.

"The best part, and I never saw it coming."

Jennifer sighed.

"We have to tell Sara."

"I know, and I know she'll think that I'm just using you, but I'm not the frivolous playboy she knew, and

I want a relationship with you, I want to see where this leads."

"We'll talk to her soon, maybe even tomorrow."

"Why so soon?"

"My trip, remember? I have to fly out on Tuesday night and won't be back for two weeks."

"I am so going to miss you, couldn't you send someone else?"

"No, I run the charity, and I have to do the negotiations."

"What's to negotiate? You're only going there to help."

"Guambi is going through a period of political upheaval since their leader died, and there is a faction there that wants nothing to do with the West, and that includes humanitarian aid."

"It's a third-world nation, Guambi is, so be careful down there."

"If they weren't poor they wouldn't need our help, and that typhoon they had devastated the country. Their people need all the help they can get."

"I wish I could go with you, but my leave ends in a few days."

Jennifer hugged him.

"We're both here now, so let's make the most of it."

Garner kissed her.

"Thank you."

"For what?"

"For giving me a chance to prove I can be trusted, I can just imagine how dire your sister's warnings were."

"Did you ever tell her about what happened to your family?"

"No, you're the first person I've told in years."

"Then, Sara never really knew you, did she?"

"No, but I know her, and if she doesn't stop her quest to get revenge, it may destroy her."

"No more talk of pain and loss," Jennifer said, and then she and Garner kissed, and the past was placed aside for the needs of the present.

CHAPTER 4 - Meet & Greet

Inside his office at the Cabaret Strip Club, Johnny had just informed Sara about the meeting he had arranged with Tanner.

They were seated on the green sofa that sat to the left side of the door, and they were the only ones in the club, early on a Saturday morning.

He had told her that Pullo had arranged a truce and that it was safe to leave the apartment, and she had agreed to do so, only because she had been going stir-crazy after staying inside for so long, but she never thought that she would be coming face-to-face with Tanner.

"He's coming here?" she said.

"Yes. He's coming here and the three of us are going to settle things peacefully. Joe said that the man doesn't want to kill you if he doesn't have to. Today, we'll make peace and you won't have to keep looking over your shoulder."

Sara took out her phone.

"I have a better idea. I'll have Duke put snipers on the roof across the street, and when Tanner shows, he's dead. What time is the meeting?"

"It's now, any minute, I told him to come at nine."

Sara's mouth dropped open and she put down her phone.

"Are you trying to get me killed?"

"I have Tanner's word that he won't hurt you, not during the meeting."

"His word? Are you serious?"

"Yes. He's a killer, but when he gives his word, he means it. Joe Pullo vouches for him and that means he can be trusted."

Sara stared at him in disbelief.

"Johnny, you're a fool, and you've just killed us both."

And as if to punctuate her words, the office door was shredded by gunfire.

***

Ten minutes earlier and a block away, Tanner had spotted the hit team as he did surveillance before the meeting.

His first thought was that Rossetti couldn't be trusted, but then realized that if Johnny had meant to double-cross him, that he would be using more than four men.

Tanner was watching the men through binoculars from the rooftop of a building that gave him a clear view of the club, and both its front and side entrances.

He had seen Johnny and Sara go into the club alone, and then spotted the four men checking their weapons in the rear parking lot of a building that was closed for the weekend.

The men all had machine pistols of some type, and were filling the pockets of their suit jackets with spare magazines.

The club was empty except for Johnny and Sara; Tanner knew it for a fact, because he had broken in earlier and checked the building out for signs of a trap.

He would trust Joe Pullo with his life, but Johnny Rossetti was a different story, and so Tanner felt the need to verify that the meeting was just a meeting.

With the arrival of the four hitters, he wasn't sure what to think. However, that changed several minutes later, as he watched the men park near the club and separate into two groups of two.

While one team picked the lock and entered quietly through the front door, the other two went to work cutting the padlock on the gate that led to the alley entrance.

That's when Tanner realized that the hit was on Rossetti, and after a moment of hesitation, he began his climb off the roof, and was crossing the street when the muffled sound of gunfire came from inside the club.

***

"It's Tanner!" Sara said, even as her ears registered that there were at least two guns firing.

Johnny pressed her down atop the sofa and shielded her with his body as a barrage of bullets continued to tear the wooden door to pieces.

When a temporary lull came, as the men outside the door reloaded, Johnny rolled onto the floor, his weapon in hand, and fired six shots at the men, seriously wounding one, while missing the other, who was partially obscured behind the first man.

The remaining man had just reloaded, and he managed to fire a shot at Johnny, even as Sara joined the battle, and after missing several shots, she caught the man with a bullet to the throat that killed him. However, when she looked at Johnny, she saw that he had been wounded, was unconscious, and had blood running down his face.

"Johnny!"

The back door to the office was kicked in and Sara turned her head to see two men taking aim at her.

Her gun arm was extended in the other direction, towards the hall, and she knew that she'd never get off a shot before they killed her.

No sooner had that thought passed through her mind when Tanner shot the men from the alley, and they crumpled to the floor, just inside the doorway to the office, each with multiple wounds.

Sara rose up, took aim at the man Johnny had shot, and who was reaching out for his fallen gun, and she emptied her last round into his chest.

"Hello, Blake," Tanner said, and Sara swung her empty gun his way.

Tanner smiled.

"I won't fall for the empty gun trick twice, and if you try to reload, I'll kill you."

"You'll kill me anyway,"

"No, I'll honor the agreement I made, now how is Rossetti doing? Is he alive?"

Sara startled, fearing her own death, she had forgotten that Johnny was wounded. She dropped back down beside him and saw that his head was resting in a puddle of blood.

"Oh no, Johnny! Wake up, can you hear me?"

After dragging the dead men farther into the office and out of the doorway, Tanner came over, and when he gazed down at Johnny, he saw the wound on his scalp.

"He was hit by a bullet. Does he have a pulse?"

Sara checked, and a few seconds later, she grinned.

"He's alive, but he has to get to a doctor."

Tanner reached down and lifted Johnny, to then carry him over his left shoulder, while keeping his gun hand free.

"Where's your car, Blake?"

Sara stepped over the bodies and followed Tanner into the alley, after closing the busted door as well as she could.

"I'm parked down here," she said, and felt surreal talking to Tanner, while knowing that he likely wanted her dead as much as she wanted to kill him, but apparently, he had taken seriously his pledge not to harm her, or so it seemed. Still, in her mind, Tanner was scum, and scum had no honor.

Tanner followed, moving slowly, while keeping an eye out for more trouble.

They reached the car without incident and Johnny regained consciousness as Tanner lowered him across the rear seat.

"Christ, my head—Tanner? Tanner, where's Sara?"

"I'm here, Johnny, I'm safe, but you need to go to the hospital."

"What happened to the two men?"

"They're dead, and there were four of them. Tanner killed the other two."

"Good man, Tanner, and no hospital, take me to the clinic, and call Joe. He has to clean up this mess."

"Am I working for you now, Rossetti?"

Johnny sighed.

"Please, I could use your help, Romeo."

"It's Tanner, and lay back and rest, that's a nasty wound you've got there. The bullet nearly split your head open."

Johnny gave half a nod and passed out again.

Sara started her car, as Tanner sat beside her in the passenger seat. He took out his phone to call Pullo, but first gave Sara instructions.

"Head to West 26th and 10th Avenue,"

"There's a doctor at this clinic?"

"The best, and the last thing Rossetti needs is the police and press sniffing around, which is what would happen if he went to a hospital."

Sara drove out the back end of the alley, and after closing the gate, Tanner returned to the car and made contact with Pullo, to fill him in. When he was done, he put the phone away and stared at Sara.

"If you're going to kill me, Tanner, please wait until after I get Johnny to the doctor."

"We have a truce, remember? I gave Pullo my word that I wouldn't harm you, not until I heard what Rossetti had to say."

Sara made a huffing sound.

"Your *word*, the word of a killer?"

"The word of a killer who just saved your life back at the club,"

"Why did you do that?"

"For Rossetti, mostly,"

"Mostly?"

"I know you hate me, Blake, but it's never been mutual, and killing your lover was nothing personal."

They were stopped at a light, and Sara turned in her seat and slapped him. The sound was loud inside the car, and the blow was delivered with force.

Tanner worked his jaw back and forth.

"I don't know what Rossetti had planned for this meeting, but you're never going to stop coming for me, are you?"

"If it is the last thing I do in this life, Tanner, I will see you dead."

Tanner was still holding his gun, and he gripped it tightly.

"You're a fool, Blake, but you do have guts."

Sara said nothing more, and other then giving directions to the clinic, Tanner remained silent as well.

CHAPTER 5 - There's a thin line...

Laurel Ivy's lovely face lit up in a huge grin when she saw Tanner, but a scowl of concern replaced the smile when she spotted the blood running down Johnny's face.

"This way," she said, and Tanner helped Johnny along. Rossetti was conscious again, but too dizzy to stand on his own.

As they walked along, Laurel examined Johnny's injury, and then introduced herself to Sara.

Sara took in the shapely, blue-eyed blonde and thought that she looked too young to have much experience as a physician.

"I'm Sara, and are you really a doctor?"

"Yes, although I've lost my license to practice."

"She knows what she's doing," Johnny moaned.

Sara looked around the clean and well-supplied medical facility, which was hidden in the rear of a small building that had an antiques store at its front end, while the clinic was separated by soundproof walls.

The building was surrounded by a fence, and there was a sign on it that listed the store's hours, but in actuality, the store never opened, and was just a facade for the illegal clinic at its rear.

There was a nurse working with Laurel, a young Asian woman named Maya, and both she and Laurel were dressed in white smocks.

Had she not known any better, Sara would have thought she was inside a big city emergency room, although the waiting room was smaller, as was the clientele.

After helping Johnny onto a table inside a treatment room, Tanner headed for the door.

"Don't you dare leave," Laurel said.

"I'll be out front. I want to make certain that we weren't followed before I go."

"Fine, but we have to talk,"

Tanner sent Laurel a nod, and then walked off.

***

Johnny had a concussion. Laurel had treated his wound, and her nurse was giving him an injection in preparation to getting a CAT Scan. While that was being done, Laurel excused herself to speak to Tanner.

Sara followed her into the hall and asked a question.

"Have you known Tanner long?"

"A few years," Laurel said.

"And are you two close?"

Laurel cocked her head.

"Are you and Tanner dating? Because I got the impression that you were with Johnny."

"I am with Johnny, but right now I'm asking about Tanner."

"Tanner and I, we have a history, but it's over and I'm with Joe Pullo, do you know Joe?"

"Yes, we've met recently, but tell me, just how close were you and Tanner?"

Laurel took a step back, and when she spoke again, her slight Southern accent seemed more pronounced.

"I'm not going to answer that, and maybe you should show more concern for Johnny. Now excuse me."

Laurel went outside and found Tanner leaning against Sara's car. She walked up to him smiling, but slapped him across the face when she reached him.

"That was for letting me believe you were dead."

Tanner shook his head in an effort to clear it.

He had been slapped twice in the last hour. Once by a woman that hated him, and now by Laurel, who supposedly loved him. The love slap hurt more.

"Knowing I was alive might have put you in danger."

Laurel wiped at tears.

"It broke my heart when I thought I might never see you again."

"Does Joe know that?"

"As a matter of fact, he does, he also knows that I love you, and he knows that you don't love me back. That's right, isn't it, that you have no feelings for me?"

Tanner sighed.

"Laurel, we had this discussion already, a long time ago."

Laurel wiped away more tears, took a deep breath, and straightened her shoulders.

"I'm going to stop making a fool of myself."

"How is Rossetti?"

"He'll be fine, but I'm giving him a CT scan just to be sure. Now tell me, what's with that woman, Sara, are you sleeping with her behind Johnny's back?"

Tanner laughed.

"That is the absolute last woman on the planet that would sleep with me. She despises me and wants me dead."

"Some say that there's a thin line between love and hate. I think I know what they mean by that when it comes to you."

"Joe's a good man, Laurel. He'll treat you right."

Laurel's gaze grew icy.

"Thank you for that advice about my love life, goodbye Tanner."

She turned to walk back inside and Tanner felt the impulse to reached out and grab her arm, to pull her back, but he stopped himself.

What else was there to say?

Laurel wanted a relationship and that was something Tanner couldn't give. He didn't need emotional complications, and in his experience, love only ended in disaster.

Laurel disappeared inside, and Sara stepped from the bathroom to gaze out at Tanner, who was walking away. She had seen the entire scene between Laurel and Tanner, before ducking out of sight, and once again she wondered if Johnny was wrong about Tanner having no weaknesses.

CHAPTER 6 - Pets or Pests

At the Cabaret Strip Club, Carl the bartender stayed near the front gate to the alley and kept watch in case anyone tried to enter it.

The clean up of the earlier firefight was going on, and Carl was glad to be nowhere near the bodies.

Carl was nervous, and his eyes roamed the street as he paced in front of the gate while tapping a hand against his thigh.

After pivoting to make a turn back the way he'd just come, he nearly collided into Tanner.

"Oh man, Tanner, please don't kill me."

Tanner reached out a hand and held Carl up, as the bartender's legs had grown weak.

"Relax Carl; I'm not here to cause trouble."

Carl began breathing again, and stood under his own power.

"Christ, how did you sneak up on me?"

"It's part of my job description, now where's Joe?"

"He's in the alley. There was a… thing here this morning."

"Four things actually, and I killed two of them, now let me by,"

Carl opened the gate and Tanner walked in.

"It's me, Joe, Tanner."

"Back here!" Pullo called out.

Tanner found Pullo standing near four body bags. When he saw Merle and Earl standing off to the side near a white van, he sent them a nod.

"What's up, boys?"

The two brothers swallowed hard but said nothing.

Pullo spoke to them.

"Why don't you two say hello, he's a friend of yours, isn't he? Isn't that right?"

Merle gestured at Tanner.

"He, we, I mean I…"

"Forget it," Pullo said, and then he pointed at the bodies. "Load those in the back of the van and then wait inside."

Merle and Earl shoved the bodies into the van, and then slunk inside the club through the back door.

When Sara informed Johnny that Tanner had been masquerading as Romeo, Merle and Earl's deception became clear.

They knew Tanner, and even if he and his Romeo disguise had fooled them initially, there was no way that the deception continued while they spent time together.

"Romeo" had also been present when Lars Gruber was reportedly killed by Tanner, who later turned out to actually be Jackie Verona, but when it came to killing, Tanner took a backseat to no one, and Pullo knew that Tanner must have killed Gruber and faked his own death by using Verona's corpse. That was why it was Jackie Verona's body unearthed with Gruber's corpse, and not Tanner, as had been originally assumed.

With Johnny's permission, Pullo interrogated the brothers, and Merle and Earl cracked immediately, begged forgiveness, and returned the reward money they'd been given.

Johnny let them live, but Pullo wanted them dead for their betrayal, and he was still pushing to be the one to do it.

"Why the hate for the Carter brothers?" Tanner asked.

"They covered for you, Tanner. We were at war with you, and they let us believe you were dead. And tell me something, why did you let them live when you knew that they could burn you?"

"I figured if they talked after all the time that had gone by, that they would be in trouble too, and besides, they're not exactly threatening."

Pullo shook his head in disgust.

"You and Johnny treat those two like pets, but they're more like pests."

"I just came from the clinic, Rossetti will be fine."

"I know, I called and spoke to Laurel, and yeah, Johnny's going to be fine, thanks to you."

"Yeah, but who were the hitters, Conglomerate boys?"

"You guessed it. Bruno Heinz can't take no for an answer."

"I could handle that problem for you and Rossetti, but first I need my own pest taken care of."

"You mean Blake? Don't worry, things are on hold for now, but Johnny will still want to sit down with you. This thing between you and his girl has to stop."

"I'm willing, she's not. The woman is obsessed with me."

"If you kill her, Johnny will come after you, and if you kill him, then, you'll have to deal with me."

"That's a lot of trouble over one woman."

"Speaking of which, how did things go between you and Laurel?"

"About the same as always,"

"Meaning?"

"Meaning that you have nothing to worry about,"

The club's head of security appeared in the doorway. His name was Bull, and he was about the size of one, with a shaved head and a scar on his left cheek.

When he spotted Tanner, he smiled.

"So Romeo is actually the great Tanner, no wonder he was such a badass."

"What's up, Bull?"

Bull gestured towards the van.

"I've got to go bury the trash. I hear we have you to thank for some of it?"

"I did my part."

"Things are a mess, and this shit has to stop. What if the club had been opened?"

Pullo slapped Bull on one of his massive shoulders.

"Things will get handled, count on it, and thanks for doing this. Do you want Merle and Earl along to help?"

Bull waved a hand back at the club.

"Let them stay, Johnny may need them later."

"Alright, and don't forget, drive slow."

"Hell yeah, I drive real slow with four stiffs in the back, take care, guys."

After the van pulled away, Pullo sent Carl inside and spoke to Tanner in front of the club.

"How do I reach you, Tanner?"

"You don't, I'll call you."

Pullo put out his hand.

"It's good to be back on the same team."

Tanner shook the offered hand, but looked doubtful.

"We'll see what happens with Blake,"

Pullo grinned.

"Are there any women you get along with?"

"I'm off to find that out. See you, Joe."

***

Inside the club, Merle and Earl sat at the bar nursing beers.

"Did you see the way Pullo looked at us?" Earl said.

Merle nodded.

"He wants us gone, and you know what that means."

"Do you think that's why Tanner is here?"

Merle laughed.

"Hell, they wouldn't pay Tanner to kill us, and besides, I think Pullo would want to do it himself."

"We gotta run, Merle, we stay here and we're dead."

"No. We stay, Pullo might want us dead, but he ain't the boss, and Johnny likes us. We just need to wait for things to cool down. If Tanner can make peace after all the guys he whacked, then we should be okay too."

"Yeah, but they need Tanner with this war startin' up, and anybody can drive a limo."

Pullo walked in and glared at them, before moving behind the bar to speak with Carl.

Earl whispered to his brother.

"We should run."

"No, I'm sick of traveling around. I like New York, like the job, and I want to stay."

"I got a bad feelin'."

"We stay. We gave back the money, Johnny likes us, and it'll be alright," Merle said, but if he had to bet on it, he wouldn't.

CHAPTER 7 - Reunited

Sophia Verona opened her front door, saw Tanner, and crossed her arms over her chest.

Tanner pointed to his right cheek.

"If you're planning on slapping me, hit me on this side, the left is getting a little tender."

"Are you going by Romeo these days, or Tanner?"

"It's Tanner, now should I stay or go?"

Sophia grabbed a handful of his shirt and pulled him towards her.

"Get your ass in here."

***

Sophia snuggled against Tanner as they lay in bed together.

"Did you miss me while you were away?"

"Yes, but it was mostly at night."

"Bastard, don't I mean more to you than sex?"

"Of course, you make great coffee too."

Sophia laughed, and then traced a finger over the wound that Sara's shot had left him with.

"This scar is new."

"Yes, I was careless."

She ran a hand through his hair.

"I like you with dark hair. The blond look never went along with those eyes of yours, and the tattoos made you look like a male bimbo."

Tanner told Sophia about the attempted hit on Johnny Rossetti, and was surprised at the level of concern he saw in her eyes.

"Is Johnny going to be alright?"

"Yes, and I see that pleases you."

"Yeah, Johnny and I broke up a long time ago, but we're still friends. It's why he sent you to protect me last month."

"Well, Rossetti has a new friend who's nothing but trouble. Have you met Sara Blake?"

"No, but I heard about her, and people aren't thrilled that he's dating an ex-Fed, and I've even heard a rumor that she was working undercover."

"No, she's an ex-Fed all right; I was there when she shot her partner."

Sophia's eyes widened in surprise,

"Why did she shoot her partner?"

"He was trying to stop her from getting revenge on me, and got shot for his trouble."

"Damn! What did you do to her?"

"I killed someone she loved. It was just business, but the woman knows how to hate."

"You're right, she sounds like nothing but trouble, but, you can't kill her. If you did, you'd have to kill Johnny too."

"I might not have a choice. The woman just keeps coming for me, and she's the reason I have this new wound."

"She shot you?"

"Yeah, I underestimated her."

Sophia scowled.

"Maybe I should kill her."

"Rossetti is trying to broker peace. I'm willing, and maybe she'll come around too."

"Don't trust the bitch."

"Don't worry, and I also want you to watch your own back. It sounds like Heinz wants a war, and that makes you a target."

"Yeah, he's slid right into Frank Richard's slot."

"For the proper fee, I'll do to him what I did to Richards."

Sophia kissed him.

"Enough shop talk; we've still got catching up to do."

Tanner's hand slipped between her thighs.

"I'll get right on that."

CHAPTER 8 - Invasion

Bruno Heinz stared out a window on the sixth and top floor of the Rutherford Hotel on Randall Street, after learning that his hit on Johnny Rossetti failed.

"Are you certain?" Heinz said to his aide, Victor, while speaking in German.

Heinz was sixty, bald, and had a big barrel of a chest, while Victor was much younger, had dark-blond hair, and was stick thin, with glasses.

"Their vehicle was found near Rossetti's tawdry club, and they have not reported in for hours. I think it is safe to assume that they were unsuccessful."

"But their last report stated that Rossetti only had a woman with him, correct? I find it hard to believe that Rossetti could triumph over a four-man team by himself."

"So do I, but, there is the rumor that the assassin Tanner is still alive, and that it was he who killed Gruber, perhaps he intervened on Rossetti's behalf."

Heinz turned from the window. The suite he was in was immaculate, large, and well-appointed. However, most of the lower floors of the Rutherford Hotel were, while functional, still under renovation, and only his people were on the premises while the work was put on hold.

"Find Tanner and make him an offer, a generous offer. If he refuses to join us, kill him."

Victor sighed.

"If he refuses, killing him could prove difficult."

"I pay you to do difficult things, Victor. Use whatever resources you need, but either recruit Tanner or kill him. Now go earn your money."

Victor bowed slightly.

"Yes sir."

After Victor left, Heinz stared out the window again, while thinking.

A few minutes later, he was on the phone with one of his people in Germany, as they spoke over a secure line.

"Send more men, Hans."

"How many, and how soon, sir?"

"A dozen by the end of the day on Monday, New York City time, and you'll have to hire mercenaries of course, but that way we won't have to concern ourselves with passports and airport security, as they'll handle that themselves, and I'll supply the weapons they'll need on this end."

Heinz could hear the man on the line take in a deep breath.

"A dozen more? So, it's war then?"

Heinz smiled.

"It will be more like an invasion."

"I'll see that it's done, and sir?"

"Yes?"

"I've located that man you wanted to speak to, Robert Vance. He's there in the city, shall I set up a meeting, or would you rather have Victor do it?"

"You do it, Victor is handling another matter."

"Fine, and I'll call you back with the details of when and where, but I take it that you won't want him at the hotel?"

"You're correct; this place needs to remain a secret. Get a time and location from Vance, and we'll discuss things in the limo."

"Fine, and sir?"

"Yes?"

"Good luck with the war."

"You have those men here by Monday night and I won't need luck, now goodbye."

Heinz put the phone away, and once again, he looked out the window, and what he saw was a city ripe for the taking.

CHAPTER 9 - The thug and the stud

The following morning, at Sara's apartment, Johnny awoke to find her in the kitchen. He was dressed in a robe, and had yet to shave.

Sara smiled when she spotted him.

"Good morning, how does your head feel?"

"I still have a slight headache, but the dizziness has passed."

"Good, and do you want coffee?"

"Yeah, and why don't we take it out on the balcony? I could use some fresh air."

"The balcony? Have you forgotten about Tanner?"

"We have a temporary truce, Sara, and if the man wanted to kill us, he could have done it yesterday."

Sara heard the logic in Johnny's words, and had already risked exposure by going out for a run earlier, because after being stuck in the apartment for days on end, she had ached to get back to her morning jog, but that didn't mean she trusted Tanner to keep his word.

"He must want something from you, likely money, but I don't believe him when he says he won't kill me. He's just biding his time. Tanner is scum, and he's devoid of honor, I can't believe you actually trust him, and have you forgotten that he killed your uncle?"

"Of course I haven't forgotten, but I have made peace with it, and in a strange way, it's one reason I trust him."

"I don't understand what you mean?"

"Richards cancelled the contract on my Uncle Al, but that didn't change things for Tanner. He had given his word to kill the man, and he carried out the hit, despite knowing that it meant he'd become a target himself. When Tanner gives his word, he means it."

"Bullshit!" Sara said.

Her phone rang, and when she checked the caller ID, she saw that it was from her sister.

"Hi Jenny."

"Good morning, Sara, and I know this is short notice, but could I stop by for a moment. I need to see you."

"That's not a very good idea, things are… unsettled in my life right now."

"I'll only stay a short while, and I'll be there in ten minutes."

"What? Jenny no, I—"

"See you soon, Sara."

The call ended and Sara stared at her phone with a furrowed brow.

"That was odd, but it looks like my sister is on her way here."

Johnny put down his cup and stood.

"I'll shave and take a quick shower, and I look forward to meeting her."

"Don't be surprised if she's not happy to see us together. You're not exactly the type of man she would pick for me."

Johnny kissed her.

"That's okay; I only care that you want me."

***

Johnny had just reemerged from the bedroom when the doorbell rang, and both he and Sara were surprised to see that Jake Garner was also visiting.

"What's going on?" Sara said.

Jennifer took Garner's hand.

"Jake and I are dating."

Sara hung her head.

"Come in out of the hall."

The couple entered and then the four of them glanced about at each other.

Jennifer broke the ice by walking over to Johnny and offering her hand.

"I'm Jennifer Blake, Mr. Rossetti."

Johnny shook her hand while smiling.

"I can see the resemblance. You're almost as beautiful as your sister."

Jennifer smiled, but Johnny saw the look of disapproval in her eyes.

"You're charming, Mr. Rossetti."

"For a thug," Garner said.

"Say what you will about him, Jake, but he doesn't sleep around behind my back. Can you say that about yourself where my sister is concerned?"

"I'm not sleeping around behind Jennifer's back. We've only been together a short time, but yes, we see each other exclusively."

"Liar,"

Jennifer went to Garner's side.

"Be quiet, Sara. You have no right to talk to him like that, and our relationship is none of your concern."

"No? Isn't that why you're here? You wanted me to see you two together, didn't you?"

"We just didn't want to keep it a secret, and of course I wanted to see you, how have you been?"

"I'm good, Jenny, and I'm actually happy these days now that I'm with Johnny."

"And... the obsession you had, about that man named Tanner. Have you given up seeking revenge?"

Sara's face reddened.

"Not revenge, justice! The man killed Brian and he needs to pay."

Jennifer looked tearful as she took Sara's hands in her own.

"Your hatred for that man is destroying you. Look at your life. You've lost your job with the FBI, you're filled with hate, and—" Jennifer glanced over at Johnny. "You're with this man, who, well I'll just say it, he's a criminal. He's the type of person that you used to place behind bars, and now you're sleeping with him? Sara, how could you?"

Sara pointed at Johnny.

"He treats me with nothing but respect, and as I said before, I don't have to worry about whose bed he's been in, I bet every time you turn your back, Jake is with another woman."

"Why? Because I couldn't possibly be enough for him?"

"I didn't say that, Jenny."

"It was implied, and I find it insulting towards both of us. Also, considering that you once almost killed him, I would think you would treat Jake better. He's been nothing but kind to you."

"I like Jake, but you two do not belong together."

Jennifer took Garner's hand.

"We're leaving."

Sara rushed over and opened the door.

"Go, but don't come crying to me when he breaks your heart."

Jennifer sniffled.

"I thought you'd be happy for me, but you're not capable of anything but anger these days, are you?"

"Righteous anger, and I'll be happy when you see Jake for what he is."

Jennifer stared at Johnny.

"I might say the same thing."

Jennifer and Garner walked out, and Sara shut the door.

Johnny exhaled loudly.

"I'm sorry that didn't go better, honey, but you can't be surprised that she doesn't approve of me."

"I don't care if she approves of you, but she should have accepted you for my sake."

"To be fair, you weren't very accepting of Mr. Fed there."

"That's different, I know Jake, and I have no doubt that he'll cheat on her and break her heart."

Johnny took her in his arms.

"Thanks for standing up for me. I'm no boy scout, but I like to think I'm not a dirtbag either."

"You're not close to being a dirtbag. It's just the opposite, and the thing I find most surprising about you, is how good you really are."

"I owe that partly to Sam Giacconi. I was just a punk when he took me under his wing, and he taught me to be a man."

"Are you and Pullo still planning to visit Giacconi later?"

"Yes, but not until the late afternoon, he usually seems more lucid then."

Sara lightly touched the bandage on the left side of Johnny's head.

"How's your wound feel?"

"It hurts, but I'm good to go."

She started unbuttoning his shirt.

"I don't know. I think we should get you back to bed."

"Ah, and will you be keeping me company?"

"Oh yes,"

Johnny smiled.

"I'm feeling better already."

CHAPTER 10 - Just how many former Navy SEALs are there?

Tanner took note when the first carload of men drove by below the speed limit, but thought nothing of it. However, when the car returned minutes later and parked three houses down, and afterwards, was joined by another one, he knew something was up.

He was at Sophia's house, after spending the night there, and the two of them were seated on her porch reading the Sunday paper.

"Sophia?"

"The two cars?"

"Yeah," Tanner said, as a smile crossed his lips. Sophia had appeared to be absorbed by what she was reading, but the woman rarely missed a trick.

"Do you recognize them?"

Sophia shook her head.

"Never saw them before, but there are four men in each of them."

The rear passenger door of the first car opened and out stepped a thin, dapper-looking man with dark-blond hair, who was sporting a pair of stylish eyeglasses that had red-tinted frames.

The man looked over at the porch for a moment before walking over slowly. His hands were extended away from his body, as if he wanted to make it clear that he wasn't armed

He looked at Tanner for just a moment, before locking eyes on Sophia. When he spoke, his English carried a strong German accent.

"Excuse me, miss, but are you Sophia Verona?"

"Yeah, that's me."

"Excellent, my name is Victor. I am associated with Bruno Heinz. You know this name, yes?"

"Yeah, but I never met him."

"It is enough that you know of him. It has come to my attention that you may be able to contact a man known simply as, Tanner. If so, please let him know that I would like to speak with him."

"What do you want to talk to me about?" Tanner said.

Victor looked at him as if seeing him for the first time.

"*You* are Tanner?"

"I am."

A smile played at Victor's lips.

"From your reputation, sir, I would have thought you to be a giant."

It was Tanner's turn to smile.

"Let me guess, you read a lot of popular fiction?"

Victor nodded.

"As a matter of fact, I do, in my off hours; I find it relaxing."

"Uh-huh, and most of the good guys and bad guys are all six-foot-six former Navy SEALs or SAS or Israeli Mossad, with genius IQ's, arms like tree trunks, and the face of a movie star. In real life, you'll find people that look like me, average-looking… but no less deadly."

Victor took a step backwards.

"Yes, as I said, your reputation precedes you."

Tanner nodded towards the cars.

"You've brought seven men with you, but I'll tell you right now, they won't be enough."

"I came here to talk, to make an offer. Mr. Heinz would like to hire you, and I can personally attest that he pays well."

"I'm not interested, no matter the price."

"Ah, that is unfortunate."

"How so?"

"I have been instructed to recruit you, and I rarely fail at a task."

"Is that a threat, Victor?"

"No, Tanner, that is a fact. Good day to both of you,"

Victor spun on his heels and walked swiftly back to the cars, where he climbed into the rear passenger seat. Seconds later, both cars drove away.

"Nervy bastard," Sophia said. "And he'll be back, count on it."

"He will be, which means I need to find a new place to stay. There's no need to drag you into this."

"I'm already in, and you're not going anywhere,"

"When they come back…"

"Yeah?"

"I'll have to kill them all."

Sophia grinned, as she recalled Victor's surprise that Tanner wasn't a giant among men.

"A runt like you, you think you can handle them?"

Tanner brought out the gun he had been holding beneath the newspaper.

"I'll manage somehow."

CHAPTER 11- The heir unapparent

Johnny and Pullo were walking towards Sam Giacconi's room, inside the care facility that housed the aged Mafia Don, when they heard laughter coming from beyond the open doorway.

When they entered, they found Sam Giacconi sitting up in bed and listening with rapt attention to a young man of twenty-two, as the man told him a humorous tale that involved much gesturing and face mugging.

Johnny stared at the kid, thinking that he looked familiar, and when he realized who it was, he was shocked by how much he had grown since the last time he had seen him.

The man's name was Sam Giacconi, called Sammy, and he was named after his grandfather.

Sammy had dark hair that he wore past his shoulders, was six-feet tall, and athletic-looking, but not thickly built. When he turned his head to take in the new arrivals, his smile lit up the room.

"Uncle Joe, and Mr. Rossetti, how's it going?"

After Johnny greeted Sam, he reached out and shook young Sammy's hand, while thinking that the kid looked a lot like his grandfather.

"Damn kid, the last time I saw you, you were a foot shorter."

Sammy grinned.

"That was a while ago, when you and Uncle Joe took me out to the range and taught me to shoot."

"Do you ever go shooting? If so, we'll go together sometime,"

"Oh yeah, I love to shoot, especially rifles."

Pullo was sitting on the edge of the bed. He pointed at Sammy with a look of pride on his face.

"The kid just graduated from college, Magna something or other, a real brain."

The elder Giacconi was having a good day, in that he remembered Johnny and Joe. That was not always the case, and they enjoyed the visit even more, as Sammy kept them laughing with his stories about life in California, where he went to college, before returning home after graduation to live with his widowed mother.

The three of them left together after Sam drifted off to sleep, and Sammy walked out to the parking lot with them, where he suddenly became serious and asked Johnny a question.

"The rumor is that The Family is going to war soon, is that true?"

Johnny looked surprised by the question, but answered it.

"Yeah, it looks that way, but that's not something you should be worried about, Sammy."

"With all due respect, Mr. Rossetti, I disagree. I'm a Giacconi, how could I not be concerned about what happens to the Giacconi Family?"

"Sam kept you out of the business after your father died, and I think I'll do the same. Use that college education, kid, get a straight job, meet a girl, have fun, and let me and Joe worry about The Family, okay?"

Sammy, whose face usually wore a smile, now darkened with anger.

"It's my family too, and yeah, my father died when the damn Russian mob tried to take over, and like him, I'm ready to defend what my grandfather built. Don't dismiss me, Mr. Rossetti; I'm not a boy anymore."

Johnny sighed.

"Look Sammy, you want in, I get that, but not now, maybe someday."

"I shouldn't even have to ask; which one of us is named Giacconi?"

Pullo pointed a warning finger at Sammy.

"This is Don Rossetti, show some respect."

Sammy looked abashed and lowered his eyes as he spoke to Johnny.

"Sorry Uncle Joe, and I apologize Don Rossetti, I meant no offense."

"Mr. Rossetti will do, and what courses did you take in college?" Johnny asked.

"I studied business technology."

"That's good, and I'm sure you can get a straight job with a degree like that."

"I'm sure I could, but I'd rather use what I know to help The Family, and that doesn't mean that I expect to start at the top. I'll start anywhere, I just want in."

Johnny placed a hand on Sammy's shoulder, and then glanced over at Pullo.

"Is there something he can do?"

"Yeah, but it's all grunt work, you know, but we do need someone in one of the chop shops, dismantling the cars that come in, that sort of thing, and in a year or two we can move him into a supervisory position."

"Are you good with your hands, kid?"

Sammy grinned.

"That's what the ladies say,"

Johnny laughed.

"Alright then, Joe will call you soon with the details, and welcome aboard."

Sammy took Johnny's hand, held it, and then leaned in and spoke in a low voice.

"I appreciate the opportunity to become a part of The Family, but I want to do more someday, especially if a war breaks out. I know the sort of work my father did, the sort of work Joe did before he became consigliere, and I want you to know, I'm ready to step into my father's shoes whenever you say so."

Johnny released Sammy's hand and stared at the young man, surprised by the request.

Sammy's father, Joseph Giacconi, who, like Joe, was named after Joe Pullo's father, had been a mob enforcer reputed to have killed over fifty men.

"Sammy, the day may come when I'll need to ask you to perform… other duties, but for now, let's see how you do at the chop shop, okay?"

"I got ya, I just wanted you to know that I'm ready and willing, Mr. Rossetti."

Sammy said goodbye to Johnny and Joe, and when he drove away in his sports car, both men waved to him from their seats inside the Hummer.

"You think the kid could take his father's place someday, Joe?"

"Yeah, Sammy is tougher than he looks, and hell, I started much younger than that, but don't worry; I'll keep him out of trouble."

"You know, that kid could be the future of The Family."

Pullo started the engine.

"It's the present I'm worried about, Heinz has to be stopped."

"Yeah, but first we have to deal with Tanner and get him back on our side, we'll need him."

"And what about Sara? Will she make peace?"

"I'll make sure of it," Johnny said, while wishing he felt as confident as he sounded.

CHAPTER 12 - Weak links

Early evening at the Cabaret Strip Club found Joe Pullo filling in for Johnny, as his boss was still recovering from his head wound.

As Pullo relaxed at the bar and nursed a beer, he kept staring at Merle and Earl, as the brothers sat at the opposite end of the bar.

His staring unnerved them and they tried not to look back, which made Pullo happy. He didn't trust the pair, and thought that Johnny was foolish not to have them killed, simply as a precaution, if nothing else.

He figured that they must overhear things while driving Johnny around, and unlike Mario, the former chauffeur, Joe believed they couldn't be trusted.

Mario died rather than betray them, and that kind of loyalty was rare.

Joe sighed. Mario had been a friend, and he missed him.

A woman walked in and all eyes turned to look at her.

That she entered the bar alone was curious enough, but her beauty and obvious grace made the eye linger.

Although it was a Sunday night, she appeared to be dressed for business, but the dark-blue pantsuit she wore did little to hide her curves, and she walked over to the bar while moving like an athlete.

Most would likely categorize her as an African-American, but she was of mixed race, and her green eyes canted slightly, while her skin appeared golden, a dark gold that glowed with health.

When she spotted him, Pullo saw a glint of recognition in her eyes and wondered why that was, but as she drew closer, he noticed two things that had escaped him earlier.

One, was that despite being fit, she was somewhere around his age, forty-one, and two, she was acting like the law, as her eyes took in everything around her.

There was a young blonde dancing on stage, and the woman stopped and gazed at her for several moments with admiration and interest, causing Pullo to wonder what team she played on.

The woman smiled at Pullo, took the stool on his right, and when Carl the bartender asked her what she would like to drink, she ordered a whiskey sour.

When the drink came, Pullo signaled to Carl that it was on the house.

The woman turned and smiled at him.

"Thank you, sir."

The voice was deeper than the voice of most women, but nonetheless feminine, and Joe found himself eager to hear her speak again.

"You're welcome, Officer, but tell me, exactly what kind of cop are you?"

The credentials came out, and the pulsating lights from the dance platform made the blue and gold badge sparkle.

Pullo read aloud the information on the card.

"Jade Taylor, Special Agent, IRS-Criminal Investigation Division,"

"And you're Joseph Pullo, a high-ranking member of the Giacconi Crime Family."

"My name is Joseph Pullo, but I'm just an assistant manager of this bar."

Jade laughed, and the sound was musical to Pullo. Had he not been involved with Laurel, he would have been tempted to find out whether he and Jade Taylor were playing on the same team, Fed or not,

"How many men have you killed Pullo?"

Pullo ignored the question and asked one of his own.

"Are you here about the mileage deductions I took on my Hummer? I assure you they were all legit."

Jade's eyes burned into his.

"I'm here because Michelle Geary was a friend of mine, FBI Special Agent Michelle Geary, a woman who was killed by your man, Mario Petrocelli."

Pullo placed his beer mug on the bar and stared at her.

"You have a vendetta against us, and you're planning on using your IRS muscle to settle the score. Go right ahead, like I said, I'm just an assistant manager, and I didn't even know your friend. What happened with Mario was a tragedy all the way around."

"Is Johnny Rossetti here?"

"He's under the weather,"

Jade stood and tossed a business card atop the bar.

"Let Rossetti know that I'm coming for him, and before I'm through, I'll see both of you behind bars for tax evasion. It's not the murder charge you deserve, but it will have to do. Goodnight, Mr. Pullo."

Pullo watched Jade walk out of the bar, and afterwards, his eyes fell on Merle and Earl again.

They were the weakest links in a chain that, if broken, could land him in a jail cell for decades. Had Michelle Geary gone after them instead of Mario, Pullo had no doubt that the brothers would have folded, worn wires, and sold anyone they could down the river to save themselves.

There was war brewing, and a Fed was gunning for them as well.

Weak links were either strengthened or replaced, but you didn't wait until they broke.

Merle and Earl had to go.

CHAPTER 13 - Give him my regards

On Monday morning, Sophia was at the kitchen sink filling the coffee pot with water, when she spotted the girl in her backyard, seated at her patio table, near the red brick grill.

"Who is that?" Sophia muttered.

She couldn't see the girl's face, but from the size and shape of her, Sophia guessed the girl was in her teens, and the way her shoulders shook, Sophia could tell she was crying.

Sophia yawned. She and Tanner had taken turns keeping watch overnight in case Victor returned with the men from the cars, and she had not gone to bed until two a.m., when Tanner took over for her.

She could hear him moving around upstairs after getting out of the shower, and figured that he would be down shortly.

The girl in the yard let out a sob, and Sophia went out her back door to see what was what, while thinking that it was probably one of the neighbors' kids who was looking for a place to go after fighting with her parents, or judging by the sobs, breaking up with a boyfriend.

"Hey honey, what's wrong?"

The girl peeked over her shoulder at Sophia and she got a glimpse of one blue eye through the strands of blond hair.

She moved closer.

"My name is Sophia. Do you live around here?"

No answer, but when Sophia moved close enough to touch her, the girl turned, and Sophia saw the gun.

"Shit!"

"That's right," the woman said, and there was the trace of a German accent in her voice.

While petite and slim, a good look at her face told Sophia that the "girl" was at least thirty, and before she could move away, the woman had the gun pressed beneath her chin.

"Call Tanner and get him out here."

Sophia was about to tell the woman what she thought of that idea when Tanner stepped out the back door and headed towards them. He was holding a gun and had it aimed at the woman.

"Shoot me and she dies," the woman said, while pressing her gun harder into the soft flesh beneath Sophia's jawline.

"What do you want?" Tanner asked her.

"There's a phone on the table, see it?"

Tanner picked up the cheap phone that was laying beside an ashtray.

"There is a number built in, call it, and that asshole Victor will have instructions for you."

Tanner did as she said, and heard Victor answer the call.

"Ah, good morning Tanner, as you can see, I am a firm believer that sometimes less is more. If I had sent a dozen men to Miss Verona's home, you might have fled, or given your skills, killed them, but a mere slip of a woman like Gerda has bested you with ease."

"I asked her and now I'll ask you, what do you want?"

"I want you, Tanner. You will leave and drive towards the main road, once there, turn right and travel past four traffic lights. Once there, you will find me and my men waiting for you in the parking lot of a boarded up building that was once a retail establishment."

"I know it. It's one light past the diner."

"Yes, excellent, now come quickly. If I do not see you in fifteen minutes, I will call Gerda and tell her to kill Miss Verona, and don't doubt that she will do it. Gerda is not a very nice person."

"And you'll also harm Sophia if I don't agree to work for you, correct?"

"Yes, she will be our guest until you perform a task for us."

"What task?"

"Johnny Rossetti, he has become a problem, but enough talk, you have fourteen minutes left."

The call ended and Tanner threw the phone atop the table.

The woman, Gerda, smiled at him.

"You should hurry, Tanner, but know this, when Victor no longer needs you, I will kill you with pleasure."

"Why?"

"Lars Gruber was my cousin."

Tanner lowered his gun, while tilting it at an upward angle.

"Tell him Romeo says hello."

The round hit Gerda in the throat, passed through, and destroyed her brainstem.

She was literally dead before hitting the ground.

Sophia staggered, and then fell on the grass beside her.

"Jesus! Tanner, that was risky wasn't it? What if her finger twitched?"

Tanner knelt down beside her.

"They weren't going to let either of us live. They just want to use me to kill Rossetti."

Sophia stood.

"Heinz really wants Johnny dead, but what do we do now?"

Tanner looked around. The yard was surrounded by an eight-foot high wooden privacy fence on three sides and couldn't be glimpsed from the street because of an equally high gate. He pointed at the body.

"Can you get rid of her?"

"Yeah, I know people, and don't worry about the neighbors calling anyone because they heard a shot. My father was as much a hardcase as you are. The neighbors know better than to call the cops."

"Good, and I'll be back soon,"

Tanner was at the gate when Sophia caught up to him.

"You're going to kill Victor and those men, aren't you?"

"Yes."

She kissed him, while being careful not to get Gerda's blood on him.

"I'll be waiting for you to get back."

Tanner nodded, opened the gate, and went off to kill eight men.

CHAPTER 14 - Confit?

Reuben Smith hated Mondays.

And to make matters worse, he had the new guy riding along with him.

The boss said the kid was old enough and had just gotten his CDL, his commercial driver's license, but the thin man named Julian looked like a teenager to Reuben's fifty-year-old eyes.

Reuben drove a dump truck, one of the huge Caterpillar models, and today he was hauling over twenty tons of gravel to a construction site in Brooklyn.

But first, he had to have his coffee.

After parking the truck in the rear of the diner, he turned to the new guy.

"I'll be right back, Julian; I'm just running in for a coffee and a cheese Danish. Do you want anything? It'll be my treat."

"No thanks, I eat Paleo."

"You eat what?"

"Paleolithic, it's a diet."

"Diet? Kid, my dick weighs more than you."

"It's not that kind of—I'm good, but thanks anyway."

Reuben grunted.

"Alright, I'll be right back, and don't change my radio station."

Reuben left the rumbling truck and headed inside, where he was pleased to see that the cute waitress was working the counter. The woman was not only good looking, but also a flirt, and although he'd never cheat on his wife, Reuben loved to flirt with the cute ones.

He was smiling at something the waitress was saying, while trying not to get caught looking down the gap in her blouse, when someone tapped him on the shoulder.

It was Julian.

The smile left Reuben's face immediately.

"What are you doing in here? And please tell me that you have the keys with you."

"He took it," Julian said, and at the same moment, Reuben caught the scent of urine wafting off him. He looked down and saw that the kid had wet himself.

"What happened? Are you sick?"

"A man, he had a gun… told me to get out of the truck."

"What man?"

***

Tanner was going over thirty miles an hour when he rammed the rear of the two cars containing Victor and his men.

Along with the twenty plus tons of gravel the truck held, its own weight, and that of its fuel, added twelve more tons to the mix.

The cars were parked in front of an old Blockbuster Video with boarded up windows, and had been facing a cinder block wall full of graffiti.

The force of the impact plowed the rear car into its companion, and the front car rocketed towards the wall and hit it with enough force to push several blocks inward.

The driver of the first car had taken off his seatbelt as he waited, and he and his front passenger went through the windshield and splattered against the wall.

Their heads had hit the cement blocks with enough force to shatter their skulls like egg shells, and their brains slid out and down into the weeds.

Tanner kept pushing after impact, and soon the front car was half its normal length, as it crumpled in on itself like an accordion, while the tires of the dump truck rolled on top of the rear vehicle, and began crushing it.

An arm brandishing a gun jutted out from a side window and pointed the weapon towards Tanner, but the limb was severed as the window frame collapsed.

Four distinct screams could be heard, but they died along with the men who made them as the truck advanced, crushed the passenger compartment, and settled atop the flattened rear car.

***

Tanner exited the truck from the passenger side, while inadvertently stepping on Julian's brown bag lunch of roasted bone marrow and carrot confit.

Traffic had all but stopped out on the highway, as everyone took in the carnage, but Tanner still had a bit of work to do before fleeing the scene.

He had a hood pulled up and wore the set of sunglasses that Reuben had left on the dash, and so very little of his features showed.

Victor was still alive in the rear seat of the first car, alive, but judging by the way the seat back had him pinned against the splintered dashboard, Tanner knew the man would not survive, and then of course, there was the matter of the fire burning under the car's hood, a fire that was spreading.

There was another survivor as well, a huge man with a piece of jagged metal through one cheek that exited out of the top of his head. There was no indication that the big man was in any pain, but his lips moved soundlessly, as his eyes blinked non-stop, and he waved bye-bye with one hand.

Tanner reached in with his knife, cut the man's jugular, and ended the show.

"Helfen Sie mir," Victor gasped out in a weak voice. It was German for "Help me."

"Wo kann ich Heinz finden?" Tanner said, as he asked for Heinz's whereabouts.

Victor appeared startled by Tanner's fluent use of German, and yet, after craning his neck to view the growing fire, he spoke in English.

"Please, Tanner, I do not want to burn to death."

"You won't, not if you give me Heinz's location."

"I want your word that you won't leave me to suffer."

Tanner lowered the sunglasses and locked eyes with Victor.

"You have my word. I won't let you suffer."

"Thank you," Victor said, and then he looked down at himself. "The odd thing is that I feel no pain, but I suppose my spine is severed down below."

"Heinz, where is he?"

"In the city, at the Hotel Rutherford, Randall Street,"

Tanner raised his gun.

"Wait! Gerda, is she dead?"

"Yes."

"Good, I never liked that little bitch."

Tanner shot Victor twice in the head, and the three men who had parked and left their vehicles to walk towards the crash, turned suddenly, and rushed back to their cars.

Tanner took off and reached the rear right corner of the property, where a rusted chain-link fence separated the lot from the row of homes behind it, where several residents were just emerging onto their porches to see what all the noise was about.

He had just made it over the fence when a police car sped into the lot. It was followed by a motorcycle cop.

The cop on the Harley spotted Tanner leaving the scene and rode over to the fence.

"Get back here!"

Tanner ignored him and just kept running, but to his surprise, the cop left his bike, tossed off his helmet, and sprang over the fence like it wasn't there.

The man was fit, fast, and wore a determined expression.

Tanner sighed inwardly.

The chase was on.

CHAPTER 15 - Rumors of war

Johnny chewed on his lower lip as he studied Jade Taylor's card.

"This is not what we needed right now."

He was inside his office at the club, sitting at his desk, and Joe Pullo was seated across from him.

The door that had been shredded by gunfire was gone, but a new one was being installed the next day, and the holes in the walls had already been patched, with new carpet put down.

The desk bore three distinct bullet holes, but Johnny had yet to replace it, while saying that they gave the desk character.

The new door would be set in a steel frame and be made of bullet-resistant glass. Anyone in the office would be able to look out into the hallway, while the other side would be mirrored. A twin of the door would also be replacing the door that led to the alley.

Pullo made a sweeping gesture with his left hand.

"My guess is that she'll start by auditing the club here; will that be a problem?"

"Not at all, I keep the club clean. I've never laundered a penny through it, and we follow every law that concerns hiring and firing. You're right though, she will start here, and so I'll call the accountants and give them a heads up."

"After the club, she'll come for you personally with that forensic accounting voodoo. If you've spent a dime more than you've declared on your taxes, she'll nail you for it."

Johnny chuckled.

"You know what's funny? I make millions every year, but the only money I spend is what I make here. It's really all I need. The rest just sits in offshore accounts earning interest under a slew of phony names."

Pullo shrugged.

"It's the same with me. Hell, my wild days are behind me. The Hummer is my only luxury, and both it and the townhouse are paid from my salary here, along with the two laundromats I own. Still, this IRS Fed will keep digging until she hits oil, and that's why we need to think ahead."

Johnny tossed the business card onto the desk.

"Think ahead how?"

"The Feds love using snitches, and those two chauffeurs of yours are ripe for the picking. She'll try to use them the same way Geary tried to turn Mario, because she'll think that they know more than they do, believing they overheard things while driving you around."

"So you're talking about whacking them again? Why do you have such a hard-on for those two; they're harmless."

"They're weak, and the weak are trouble. Look, personally, I can take them or leave them, but they knew that Tanner was alive and said nothing. What if Tanner had still wanted to kill you? You'd have never seen it coming."

Johnny gazed out the open doorway, and at the other end of the hall, he could see Merle and Earl seated at a table and playing cards. The bar wasn't open for business yet, and the boys were just hanging out in case Johnny needed them.

"Let me think about it."

"Don't think too long, or Jade Taylor might get her hooks into them, but now tell me, what's the story with Tanner? Are you still trying to make peace between him and Sara?"

"Yeah, Tanner is coming by later."

"He called you?"

"No, Sophia called me last night to see how I was doing, and Tanner is staying with her. Apparently, those two have a thing going."

"What time is he coming by?"

"Around six, and Sophia wants to sit in, so you might as well too."

"Good, but Sara doesn't know that he'll be here, does she?"

"No, but she's meeting me here so that we can go out to dinner together, and when she shows, I'll try to make peace."

"If she won't let her vendetta go, things are not going to end well."

"Maybe, or maybe she'll kill Tanner."

"Even if she did, we'd be in trouble. We could use Tanner if a war broke out."

Johnny grimaced.

"What's that face for?" Pullo asked.

"Tanner, Sophia said a guy named Victor came to see Tanner yesterday. It looks like Heinz wants to recruit him. What do you think, would Tanner switch sides?"

Pullo laughed.

"Tanner doesn't have a side. He just kills who he's paid to kill."

"Like my uncle?"

"That still burns you, doesn't it, that he killed Al?"

"Yeah, but my uncle knew the rules just like we all do, and it's better to have Tanner on your side than against you. So, I'll just live with it."

"If your girl would take that attitude we'd all be a lot better off."

"Sara is intense, and she tends to see the world in black and white. She's already made a major change by being with me. Before we got close, I was just another mobster to her, a bad guy, and to her, Tanner is the worst of the worst."

"He's actually the best of the best, which is why we need him on our side, but if things don't go well at this meeting, and he kills Sara, what will you do?"

"I'd kill him, Joe. Sara means a lot to me."

"You'd lose, and then I would go after him... and as much as I hate to admit it, I'd lose, and then Heinz would just waltz in and take over everything without firing a shot."

Johnny hung his head.

"Sara has to make peace with Tanner, or... we could double-cross him at this meeting."

Pullo tensed as he raised an eyebrow.

"I gave him my word, Johnny. If you go that route, count me out of it."

Johnny waved a hand in the air.

"That was desperation talking. It's like Sam always says, if you can't trust a man's word, he's not a man."

Pullo relaxed again and settled back in his seat.

"We'll get Tanner and Sara together and see what happens, but if I know Tanner, he's got plans of his own."

"What's that mean?"

"We need him and he knows it. If we can't work things out, there's always the chance he could go to work for Heinz."

The phone rang. When Johnny looked at the caller ID, he saw that it was Sophia.

The call was short, the words spoken in code phrases, but Johnny understood that Heinz had made a move on Tanner that backfired. When he ended the call, Johnny was smiling.

"What did Sophia have to say?"

"You don't have to worry about Tanner working for Heinz, and if I understood correctly, Tanner has already started on thinning his troops."

Pullo laughed.

"Let me guess, Heinz tried to control Tanner?"

"Yeah, I guess he didn't learn anything from watching Frank Richards make that mistake."

"Where is Tanner now?"

"She didn't say, but I guess he's out on Staten Island somewhere."

"Tanner and Sophia, now there's a combo,"

"Think it will last?" Johnny said.

"No, I don't think Tanner is capable of falling in love," Pullo said, and then he thought about Laurel, and hoped that he was right.

CHAPTER 16 - Catch me if you can

The cop was relentless.

And worse, the cop was gaining on Tanner. After climbing over the fence upon leaving the scene where he killed Victor and his men, Tanner had run through a quiet neighborhood without seeing anyone, other than the few people who stood in their doorways wondering about the noise, or those passing by in cars.

He could hear the cop shouting his description and location into a radio as he ran, and knew that others would join the chase within minutes, if not seconds.

What had been a good lead had shrunk considerably, as the cop's longer legs propelled him ever closer.

The man was in shape, as was Tanner, but unlike Tanner, time was on the cop's side.

After reaching the next intersection, Tanner turned right and saw the entrance to a cemetery across the street and half a block away.

He headed for it, with the hope that by weaving around the mausoleums and statuary, that he could put more distance between himself and the cop.

A minute later, he knew the plan wouldn't work, as the cop reacted quickly and mirrored his every turn, while still managing to grow closer to him.

At the exit on the other side of the property, Tanner cursed as he ran by an idling pickup truck that had the name of the cemetery stenciled on its side.

The truck was just sitting there ready to be driven away, but the cop was so close behind him that Tanner realized he would never have enough time to climb inside it, much less place the vehicle in gear, before the cop could just yank him out of it.

He ran on after leaving the cemetery, and a block later, they left the neighborhood and emerged onto Victory Boulevard. There were people everywhere, and most of them did a double take as Tanner sprinted past them.

One of the stores was selling fruit, and as Tanner ran by, he snagged an orange from atop a crate that was full of them, and which was set up outside the store to display them, along with other fresh produce.

The store owner had been standing nearby, and he rushed onto the sidewalk to yell at Tanner, and did so, just as the cop reached the same spot, and it was only the cop's quick reflexes that saved him from a full-on collision with the man.

The store owner was still spun around after being hit on the arm by the cop's right hip, as the officer swiveled away from him, but his nimble avoidance of disaster had still caused the cop to stumble and slow down, and Tanner once again had a decent lead.

He planned to put it to good use, along with the orange he carried.

In the distance, Tanner could just make out flashing lights approaching through the heavy morning traffic, and knew that he had to do something quick.

When he reached the next corner, he saw an apartment building down a side street on his right and, after crossing the street, he headed for it.

He had been prepared to kick in the door, but the front door was unlocked, and when he rushed inside, he saw exactly what he'd hoped to see, a staircase.

Tanner forced himself to wait a few seconds before taking action, and gulped in as much air as he could while doing so.

If he acted too soon, what he had planned would be useless. When he could hear the cop's footfalls outside, he tossed the orange up so that it would go over the banister and fall upon the next flight of stairs.

With adrenaline flowing through his veins, he did even better than he had hoped to, and the orange fell atop the stairs leading up to the third floor.

With that done, he hurried over to an alcove where a baby carriage was parked, and slid out of view beside it, and did so just as the cop rushed into the vestibule.

Tanner's eyes watered as he stifled his gasps for breath while hearing the cop's deep breathing, but it was the second sound that pleased him, the sound of the orange, as it rolled and thumped its way back down the stairs.

It wasn't the sound of footsteps, but it was a sound, and it was enough to make a keen pursuer take notice.

The cop fell for it, went bounding up the stairs to hunt for his man, and as soon as he hit the landing and started up the second flight, Tanner left the alcove and went back outside, while shedding the hoodie and removing his gloves and sunglasses.

The hoodie was black, but the T-shirt beneath it was white, and although not a disguise, it was a stark contrast.

Tanner shoved the hoodie down a sewer drain, grabbed the crumpled newspaper that had been blown into the gutter, and walked back to Victory Boulevard, where he discovered that the distant flashing lights were just a block away, and slowing to make the turn.

He opened the newspaper, leaned back against a wall, and attempted to look casual.

The patrol car nearly overshot its turn, but corrected and came to a screeching halt in front of the apartment building. It was joined just seconds later by two more units, which had arrived from the other direction.

Tanner tossed the newspaper in the trash can of a donut shop and then went inside to buy a coffee, while also buying Sophia a chocolate chip muffin, which was her favorite.

Two minutes later, he was in a cab headed back to the parking lot of an auto parts store where he had left his car. The store was on the highway, next to the diner where he had made Julian's acquaintance and stolen the truck.

By the time he returned to Sophia's, Gerda's body was gone, and Sophia was watching the aftermath of his hit on Victor and the other seven men on the TV in the kitchen.

She sent him a sideways glance.

"Remind me to stay on your good side."

The TV showed an aerial view of the carnage he had inflicted with the dump truck, but soon switched to a different chopper, and this one hovered above the apartment building near Victory Boulevard, where several patrol cars were gathered.

The hosts of the program speculated over the significance of the cop who emerged from the building holding an orange in an evidence bag, and even had the camera zoom in on the man.

Sophia nodded at the TV.

"That cop with the orange is cute."

Tanner tore a small piece off her muffin.

"And fast too,"

CHAPTER 17 - Peace in our time

Unlike Sophia, Bruno Heinz wasn't watching TV; he was on the phone, and getting more frustrated by the second at his inability to reach Victor.

Finally, after numerous attempts, he instructed one of his other aides to track down Victor. That also proved futile, however, it did result in Heinz learning that not only was Victor not answering his phone, but neither were any of the men he'd taken with him.

When he learned that Victor had also hired an independent contractor named Gerda to assist, and that she too was not answering or returning calls, he came to understand that Tanner's reputation was well-earned.

Within minutes of that realization, he was on the phone to Germany again.

"Yes sir?"

"Have you secured the men yet?"

"I have, and they will all be arriving in New York over the next twelve hours."

"Excellent, also, contact our Hungarian friend."

"The Hungarian? Yes sir, but may I remind you of his fees, they are very—"

"Expensive, yes, but also worth the cost, his team of assassins has never failed."

"True, but is the expense necessary? Is Mr. Rossetti that formidable?"

"I don't need them to kill Rossetti; I need them to kill a man named Tanner. I had hoped to have him work for me, but he's chosen a different path, and now it's time he learned that he is not the only deadly man for hire."

"The Hungarian's team consist of four men; this man Tanner will be dealt with swiftly."

"Yes, and Hans?"

"Yes sir?"

"Hand over your responsibilities there to your immediate subordinate and come here by the end of the week, you will be moving up and taking over Victor's duties."

There was a pause, as the implications of that request sank in.

"I'm honored by the promotion, but also saddened, Victor was a friend."

"Tanner killed him, along with several others."

"In that case, sir, I will be personally adding on to the fee you'll be paying the Hungarian."

"Why?"

"I understand that for a price, the target will be tortured before being killed, and I would like this Tanner to experience that agony, in memory of Victor."

Heinz smiled into the phone.

"Hans, you and I are going to work well together, now get busy completing your instructions, and by tomorrow evening, Tanner will be dead."

***

Heinz wasn't the only one who wanted Tanner dead, and later that day, when Pullo escorted Tanner and Sophia into Johnny's office, Sara stared daggers at him from where she sat beside Johnny, behind his desk.

Pullo stayed for the meeting, and stood at Tanner's left, while leaning against the wall.

"I want you to know that this meeting wasn't my idea," Sara said. "I don't want peace. I want you dead."

Tanner looked back at her, but said nothing, while Sophia walked over and glared down at Sara.

"The man Tanner killed, the one you want revenge for, he was a member of The Conglomerate, right, he worked for Richards?"

Sara looked her up and down.

"Who are you?"

"I'm Sophia Verona, now answer my question."

Sara huffed, but did answer.

"The man Tanner killed was named Brian Ames, and yes, he worked for MegaZenith, but when he found out what was going on, he contacted the FBI, and that's when we met."

"So he told you that he was just an innocent little lamb, is that it? Well, let me tell you something, lady, no one had access to anything in The Conglomerate unless they knew the code to the encrypted files. We confiscated Richards' computers after his death and my people still can't crack the code, so if this Brian had access or was in the inner circle, he was no innocent, and if he turned snitch, then he just got what he had coming."

Sara's face went red, and she stood. Both she and Sophia were tall for women, and they appeared to be the same height.

"Tell me one more time how Brian deserved to die and I will rip the hair from your head."

Sophia started to respond, but Tanner held up a hand and everyone looked at him.

"We're here to end a problem, not to start a new one, and while Sophia was right about Ames not being an innocent, that has little to do with why we're here today."

Sara shook her head.

"She was wrong about Brian, and she's also wrong about Richards' files being inaccessible, because you have access to them, don't you Tanner?"

Tanner held back his surprise at Sara's knowledge, but couldn't hold back his smile; the woman was not only tough, but sharp. She knew that Al Trent had been in Ridge Creek because she had tracked his phone there, and from that knowledge, she must have extrapolated that Tanner used Trent to access Richards' files. And while her facts were faulty, her conclusion was correct.

Johnny asked Tanner and Sophia to take seats in front of the desk, and then followed up on Sara's hunch.

"Does the name Tim Jackson mean anything to you, Tanner?"

"It does, and so you know I'm not bluffing. I have the same files as Jackson. Those files are keeping him safe, and they'll also get me what I want."

"How so?" Johnny said.

Tanner gestured at Sara.

"She backs down or I hand the files over to the IRS." Tanner plucked Jade Taylor's card from atop Johnny's desk, "And I see that they're already sniffing around."

Pullo spoke up.

"What's in the files, financial records?"

Johnny answered.

"Judging by what Jackson sent me, there's every transaction made between the Giacconi Family and MegaZenith since the beginning of The Conglomerate, along with the names of the dummy corporations we used, and while none of it would touch us personally, it would give the government cause to close down everything and seize all assets."

Tanner stared across the desk at Sara.

"I'm giving you a chance to end this without bloodshed, Blake. Agree to back down or I'll destroy your boyfriend's business, and if you keep coming after that, I'll kill the both of you."

Pullo sprang from the wall, walked over, and stood beside Tanner, to glower down at him where he was seated.

"If you were anyone else, I'd have killed you just now for making that threat."

"If I was anyone else, you would succeed, try it with me and I'll put you in traction."

Pullo's hands balled into fists.

"Goddamn it, Tanner, don't test me."

"I'm tired of playing games with this woman, Joe. Either she backs off or things go very badly. There's no middle ground."

"Even if I agree to let things be, why should we trust you?" Sara asked.

"Because I would give you my word,"

Sara laughed.

"The word of a scumbag, a killer for hire? What's that worth? Nothing, that's what it's worth. And another thing, why would you trust me?"

Tanner shrugged.

"You've never lied to me, not once, not even when I stood in your apartment holding a shotgun on you, you just got in my face and told me that you would see me dead someday."

Sophia turned her head and stared at Tanner.

"You two were alone in her apartment?"

Sara made a face.

"Please, I'd rather sleep with a dog than ever touch Tanner."

Sophia smiled.

"You don't know what you're missing."

Johnny squirmed in his seat.

"Let's stay on topic. Tanner is willing to make peace, and he'll trust Sara to keep her word, that's good, that's a start."

"It's not my word you have to worry about," Sara said. "And why should I back down? I damn near killed you in Pennsylvania, Tanner; maybe next time I'll get it done."

"I underestimated you, Blake. I admit that, but I won't do it again, and if we don't reach an agreement today, I promise you, you'll be dead by the end of the week."

Johnny pointed a finger at him.

"Anything happens to her, and I will kill you."

"No, Rossetti, you'll try, and then I'll kill you." Tanner tossed a thumb at Pullo. "After that, Joe will come, and I'll kill him. The three of you will be dead, and I'll talk business with whoever replaces you. You see, you were wrong when you said that I'm here to make peace.

I'm not here to make peace; I'm here to give you a chance to save your lives."

Sara looked at him with disgust.

"You arrogant, condescending piece of shit, you really think you're something special, don't you?"

"No, Blake, but I'm better at killing than anyone has ever been, and it's a skill I don't mind using."

"Johnny," Sophia said.

"What?"

"Take the deal, Tanner won't say it, but I will. He likes you, and the only reason he agreed to this meeting is because you've hooked up with her. If not for you, he would just kill her, and if she got lucky and killed Tanner, then, I would kill her, hand to God."

Johnny stared across at Tanner for a few moments before turning to Sara.

"I understand wanting vengeance, but I don't see any way for this to end well. Please, make peace with the man and give him your word that you'll back off."

"And I'm supposed to take his word as well?"

"His word is good. He came here to talk like he said he would, and we both know that he could have killed you the day we were attacked, but he didn't, because we had a temporary truce. Tanner will keep his word."

Sara shook her head.

"He can't be trusted."

"He can," Johnny said, as he reached over and took her hand. "Make peace, baby, I couldn't bear to lose you."

Sara squeezed his hand, gritted her teeth, and nodded.

"I promise not to try to kill Tanner, but mark my words, the man can't be trusted, and the second he goes back on his word, all bets are off."

Tanner stood, and Sophia followed suit, then, Johnny stood and offered his hand, and he and Tanner shook.

"Now that we've made peace, let's discuss war. Heinz won't quit coming after either of us."

"Is that a job offer?" Tanner said, "Because if it is, my price will be high."

Pullo gestured towards the doorway, which still sat open while awaiting its new door.

"If you ladies will excuse us, we won't be long, have a drink at the bar."

Sara stood, her gaze still one of stone as she looked at Tanner, but she walked past him without a word and headed down the hallway.

Sophia chuckled.

"I'll go keep the bitch company, maybe she'll loosen up after a couple of drinks."

"Be nice," Johnny said, and Sophia smiled sweetly over her shoulder as she left the room.

With the women gone, the men sat once more, with Pullo taking the seat vacated by Sara.

"How high a price are we talking, Tanner?" Johnny asked.

"Three times my old rate; I think the last few months have proven I'm worth it."

Joe whistled.

"That's a nice fee."

"There's more, I also want fifty K just to sign on."

Johnny wagged a finger at him.

"That's a lot of money."

"And you'll get a lot for it. Heinz will regret ever leaving Germany."

"That thing with the dump truck this morning, that was you, wasn't it?" Johnny said.

"It was, and Heinz lost eight men."

"He'll send more," Pullo said.

"He will, and they'll die too, or, I can take Sophia and head off for a vacation. So what will it be Rossetti, do I have a job or not?"

Johnny stared at Tanner, as he thought things over. When he came to a decision, he made a nearly imperceptible nod.

"You're hired, and call me Johnny, hell, you've already saved my life twice."

Tanner stood.

"You'll get your money's worth, don't worry."

"And Sara, I have your word that you won't hurt her?"

"Yes."

Johnny made a sigh of relief.

"Good, she needs to put her old life in the past and move on."

Tanner sent a nod to Pullo and headed towards the doorway.

"One more thing, Tanner," Johnny said.

"What's that?"

"The Carter brothers, do you care what happens to them?"

Tanner raised an eyebrow.

"Did the boys get on your bad side?"

"Not me, Joe here, he doesn't trust them,"

Tanner shrugged.

"I've nothing against them, but Joe's instincts are good. Do what you will with them."

"Fine, and I'll be in touch."

Tanner left, and Johnny turned to Pullo.

"Merle and Earl, they're in your hands now; do what you think is right."

"Thanks, and I get no pleasure from it, but yeah, they have to go."

"When?"

"I'll do it tomorrow. I'll take a little ride in the limo with the boys... and come back alone."

Johnny sighed.

"What?"

"Those two, they kind of grew on me,"

"Like fungus," Pullo said, and then he headed out into the bar.

CHAPTER 18 - Wrapped to go

Inside the Cabaret Strip Club, Sara and Sophia sat in the roped-off VIP area at the side of the bar, while having a drink.

The area could be curtained off from the rest of the room, and had its own small stage with a pole in the middle, but neither the pole nor the stage was in use.

Sara studied Sophia over the rim of her glass, and asked a question.

"How long did you and Johnny date?"

"A little over two years,"

"Really? It sounds like you were serious."

"We were, and even talked about getting married, but we were just kids then too,"

"And you and Tanner, is it serious?"

Sophia narrowed her eyes.

"Why all the questions?"

"I'm curious. Why would you be with Tanner when you know what he is?"

"Yes, I know what he is, but you're confusing that with what he does. My father was Jackie Verona, and he killed dozens of men, same as Tanner, and let me tell you something, my father was a good man, and a great father."

Sara smiled.

"Ah, I see, you have daddy issues. That's why you're with Tanner; he reminds you of your father."

"You bitch! Who the hell are you to psychoanalyze me? Keep talking shit and I'll—"

Tanner appeared and took Sophia's hand.

"Say goodbye to your new friend, we're leaving."

"Friend my ass, I see why you wanted to kill her."

"C'mon, I'll take you to dinner, goodbye, Blake."

"Goodbye, Tanner, and don't for a second think that you're fooling me. Johnny may trust you, but I never will."

"Right, just keep your word and we won't have a problem," Tanner said, and then he and Sophia headed for the door.

As they passed him, a man seated at the main stage stood and followed after them, but before he did so, he sent Sara a nod. The man was Duke.

Sara intended to keep her word, but was not going to be unprepared when Tanner broke his, and he would break it, of that she was certain, and Duke would insure that she wasn't caught unawares.

Sara ordered another drink, and when it came, she said a silent toast to Brian Ames, her dead and still mourned lover.

***

At that moment, in Brooklyn, Bruno Heinz was meeting with Robert Vance.

They were inside Heinz's limo, parked near the famous Brooklyn Heights Promenade, but neither man was interested in taking in the spectacular view of Manhattan.

Vance was in his early-thirties, blond, tall, and had light-blue eyes. He was Russian by birth and upbringing, but like Tanner, he spoke many languages, such as English, which he spoke without a trace of an accent.

He was a trained assassin, and a former member of Russia's Federal Security Service, an organization once known as the KGB.

"Tanner killed Richards and ruined the man's plans, and I hope you understand, Heinz, Richards' plan to kill you and the others was his idea, not mine. I simply carried out his orders."

A small smile formed on Heinz's lips.

"I understand, as a young man, I too took orders, some of which I didn't like, but that is the past, and if you're willing, I would like your help."

"You're planning to step into Richards' shoes?"

"A crude saying, but yes, in essence, that is what I am doing, and I can use a man with your skills."

"You want me to kill Tanner?"

Heinz looked startled by the question.

"Do you think that you could?"

"Absolutely, I'm every bit as good as Tanner, and I would love the chance to prove that I'm better."

"You may be up to the task, but I have a team of men coming here to solve that problem."

"What men, Mercs?"

"Yes, but not just any mercenaries. These men work for a man named Magyar, a Hungarian who lives in Brussels."

"Boldizsár Magyar? I know him well, I was once a member of an earlier team of his, as was Lars Gruber, and yes, his men will not be ordinary mercenaries."

"No, they will not be, and they will kill this man Tanner, and once they do, that is when I will need you, as I take over and control this city."

"Once Rossetti is dead, the rest of the families will fall easily, but Rossetti is protected by a man named Pullo, and Pullo is loyal to Rossetti. I suggest you remove him as well."

Heinz smiled.

"Good advice, and I assume we have a deal?"

"Yes, I'll join you, and if Magyar's men don't kill Tanner, he's mine, agreed?"

Heinz laughed.

"Agreed, but really, what are the odds of Tanner defeating such men?"

Vance frowned.

"Not good, knowing Magyar, each man on that team will be exceptional, still, if Tanner survives, I want my shot at him."

"It's a deal. Now, let's discuss your compensation."

***

Tanner took Sophia to dinner, where they talked over the day's events.

"You know that Heinz will be sending more men after you, don't you?"

"Of course, it was why I asked you to pack a bag. I have to work tonight, and I didn't want to leave you alone at your house."

Sophia pouted.

"I thought we were staying at a hotel for a night of romance, now you tell me that I'll be there all by myself."

"It can't be helped, as you said, Heinz will be sending more men after me, and he'll likely be importing."

"So?"

"I want to welcome them to the city, my way."

Sophia grinned.

"Oh God, I can only imagine what that means, but please, baby, be careful."

"I'll do my best," Tanner said.

Sophia looked around the restaurant and spotted a friend she knew who was an actress on Broadway. The woman had been on her way out the door with a large group of people, but when she spotted Sophia, she smiled wide, put her hand to her ear and made the gesture that said, "Call me."

"Your friend looked familiar," Tanner said.

"She should, that's Amber Rose, she won a Tony last year, but you probably remember her from those insurance commercials she used to do. We grew up on the same block, and she used to date my brother."

"About your brother,"

"Yeah?"

"I was surprised by what you said about snitches when you were talking to Blake, given that Lars Gruber killed him for talking to the Feds."

Sophia gave a little shrug.

"Tony turned snitch to help save our father, and he knew he'd pay for it. What Blake doesn't get, is that you didn't kill that Brian Ames for the hell of it, you did it because you were hired to do a job. Ames killed himself when he talked, and so did my brother, the difference is, Tony did it to save our father, who knows why Ames did it."

Dessert came, and Sophia downed a piece of chocolate cake while sighing in pleasure, when she was finished eating, she moaned.

"When you return to the hotel tomorrow, look for me in the fitness center. It'll take me hours to burn off that cake, but oh, was it worth it."

"I don't have to leave right away, and I have a little fun planned, something I could use your help with."

Sophia smiled.

"What sort of fun?"

Tanner smiled back at her.

"I need to send someone a message."

***

Sara and Johnny also went out to dinner, while Joe Pullo stayed late at the club.

Afterwards, they went to a bar in Midtown that featured live jazz. Sara felt good to be out on the town, after being fearful of leaving her apartment for so long, but eventually she and Johnny returned there.

Johnny began kissing Sara as she opened her apartment door, and just seconds after closing it behind them, they were on her sofa locked in a passionate embrace.

When things escalated to the point that Sara's dress laid on the floor and Johnny was shirtless, Sara stopped him from removing his pants and whispered in his ear.

"Take me to the bedroom."

Johnny swooped Sara up in his arms like a bride and carried her down the hallway, and as they walked along, he used his teeth to slide one of her bra straps down along her arm, causing her to giggle.

However, the giggle died in her throat, when they heard the moan come from beyond the open bedroom door.

Johnny stopped suddenly, lowered Sara's bare feet to the carpet, and reached down to free the gun from his ankle holster.

"Who's in there?" Johnny demanded, but was answered by another low moan.

After gesturing for Sara to stay back, he got down low, and peeked around the doorframe.

"What the hell…?"

Duke lay atop the bed, wrapped in duct tape from head-to-toe, with only his nose and eyes uncovered.

Johnny entered the bedroom with Sara following behind, and plucked off the note that was taped to the headboard.

DON'T PRESS ME, BLAKE. LET IT GO! - TANNER

Sara looked up at Johnny with a guilty gaze.

"I don't trust Tanner, and Duke was just following him."

Johnny paced for a moment, opened his mouth, but said nothing, and then stormed from the room, with anger radiating off of him like steam from a pipe.

Sara sighed as she watched him leave, and then she bent over the bed and tore the tape away that was covering Duke's mouth.

"Did you plant the device before Tanner caught you?"

Duke didn't answer; he was busy staring at Sara's breasts, which were practically spilling out of a red lace bra just inches from his face.

She made an exasperated sound, straightened up, and reached down and tapped him on the cheek.

"Duke?"

"Sorry honey, but I am a man you know, and yes, I planted the tracker. Now you'll know where Tanner is at every moment."

Sara grinned.

"And knowing where he is, I can kill him."

CHAPTER 19 - Words fail him

On East 38th Street, Tanner rang the doorbell that belonged to Laurel Ivy.

The lights were on in the townhouse, and he assumed that she was staying up late to greet Pullo when he returned from the club.

Sophia was tucked away safely in a 5-star hotel, but after visiting Laurel, Tanner would be visiting another hotel, The Hotel Rutherford, where Bruno Heinz was headquartered.

Laurel opened the door after checking through the peephole, and her large blue eyes were full of questions.

"Why are you here, Tanner?"

"May I come in?"

Laurel hesitated for only a second, and then bid Tanner to enter.

His pulse was elevated once more at the sight of her, and he inwardly cursed whatever caused the reaction. However, every time he saw her, it was like seeing the sun for the first time.

"The men who hurt Rossetti the other day, they worked for a man named Heinz, and it's possible that the Giacconi Family will be going to war with him."

"That's disturbing, but why are you telling me that?"

Tanner handed her a strip of paper.

"You can reach me at that number. If anything happens, if you even think you're in danger, call me."

Laurel looked down at the paper, and as she did so, Tanner studied her. She wore no makeup, was dressed in a pink robe with matching slippers, and her jewelry had been removed in preparation for going to bed.

Tanner had seen Laurel only briefly since the days when they were lovers, but he thought that she was more beautiful than ever, and he actually had to stop himself from reaching out to caress her blond curls.

Laurel looked up at him.

"Why would you give me this? I know you don't care about me. You made that clear years ago when you left me."

"You were married."

Laurel moved closer, and Tanner inhaled the scent of her, an aroma like roses that was likely just her shampoo or soap, but nevertheless, he found it intoxicating.

"I know I was married, and yes, I cheated on my husband with you, but it was because I loved you the moment I saw you. Was I a complete fool? Were you just using me for sex and a good time? If that's the truth, I can hear it, and I'd rather live with the truth than mourn for a lie."

Tanner blinked rapidly.

"It's not true. I never used you; it's just that... you wanted too much. You wanted something that I couldn't give."

Laurel touched him on the cheek.

"I just wanted to hear you say you loved me, and you did love me, didn't you? I was so certain back then, I could see it in your eyes, feel it in your touch, and you laughed back then, we laughed every time we were together, we were so happy, Tanner, so goddamn good together... and then you just walked away."

Tanner looked down at the floor.

"I can't give you what I don't have, and I walked away so that I wouldn't hurt you anymore than I already had."

Laurel lifted his chin with a gentle hand and stared into his eyes.

"You weren't afraid of hurting me. You were afraid of being hurt *by* me. Love scares you to death, doesn't it?"

Tanner backed away and let her hand fall.

"None of that matters anymore. What happened between us was years ago, and you're with Joe now."

Tanner headed for the door and Laurel called to him, when he turned to look back at her, he saw that she was wiping away tears.

"Just tell me one thing, please?"

"What?"

"You did love me, didn't you? You couldn't say it then, but please say it now, I so need to hear it."

Tanner swallowed the lump that was suddenly in his throat, and pointed at the slip of paper he'd given Laurel.

"Don't lose that, and I'll be there if you need me, now goodbye."

Tanner opened the door and stepped out into the night, to rush away from a woman that loved him, and towards men who wanted him dead.

Their hate was far easier to deal with than her love.

CHAPTER 20 - Fool me once...

After putting on a robe, Sara returned to the bed and started tearing at the tape covering Duke.

"How did Tanner wrap you up so much by himself?"

"He wasn't alone; he was with that redhead, Sophia. She was actually the one who hit me with a stun gun as I was getting in my van."

"That bitch, but tell me, you saw them together, do you think he cares for her?"

"Yes, but I don't think he loves her, and if you think threatening her would make him give up, you'd be wrong."

"I agree, but damn it, the man must have a weakness."

"And if you find it, what then?"

Sara stopped tearing at the tape and straightened up.

"I won't go back on my word, I never have, but I have to be prepared when Tanner goes back on his. I know the man, he's as devious as they come, and if I have any hope of surviving him I'll need leverage, but tell me, how did you plant the tracking unit?"

"Tanner did it himself, that's how they're designed. I broke into his car and placed it on the brake pedal. The second he stepped on it, it became embedded in the bottom of his boot."

"Won't it just fall off?"

"No, he would have to cut it out. This is real hi-tech spy stuff, ha, and wait until you see the bill for the tiny little bugger."

"Where's the tracker?"

"There's no device, just a satellite link, and I sent you the code by email. You can even install it on your phone as an App."

Duke's hands were free, and he tore away the last of the tape.

"God that hurts, and I won't have any arm hair for a while."

Sara patted him on the shoulder.

"This was risky, but you did it, and I'll show my appreciation with a bonus."

"Thanks, but you better go talk to that boyfriend of yours. He looked really pissed."

"He'll calm down, and once I prove to him that Tanner can't be trusted, he'll thank me."

***

Sara found Johnny putting on his suit jacket as he prepared to leave the apartment.

"Where are you going? I thought you were staying?"

"And I thought you could be trusted,"

"What's that mean? I said that I wouldn't try to kill Tanner, I never said that I wouldn't have him followed."

Duke came out of the bedroom, looking disheveled, and a bit sheepish.

"I still can't believe Tanner spotted me following him. I must be getting old."

Johnny shook his head in disgust.

"You're lucky he didn't kill you, and if he had, I wouldn't blame him. Tanner is not a man you want to play games with."

Duke opened the door.

"I'll leave you two alone. I have to go home and soak this glue off my skin, goodnight."

Duke left, and Johnny placed his hand on the door to leave as well, but stopped when Sara hugged him.

"Don't go. I know you don't agree with what I did, but I don't trust Tanner, and I'm surprised that you do."

Johnny took his hand off the door and went over and sat on the sofa. When Sara sat beside him, he spoke to her.

"Tanner killed my Uncle Al, you know that of course, you were there, but did you also know that when Richards cancelled the hit, he told Tanner that he could keep the fee?"

"I was aware of all that, but so what? You think that Tanner ignored Richards and killed your uncle out of a sense of honor, out of a need to keep his word? Because, if that's what you think, you're wrong, Tanner has no honor, just a need to kill, a desire to outsmart everyone, and by pretending to want to make peace with me, he's outsmarted you."

"How do you figure that? If he wanted us dead he could have stayed here after dropping Duke atop the bed, and killed us as we walked in the door."

"He won't be that obvious. He wants me dead, but he doesn't want you or Pullo coming after him, and so my guess is that he's planning on making my death look like he had nothing to do with it, either that, or he'll remove you from the equation first, and in a manner that won't make Pullo suspicious."

"That sounds too sneaky for Tanner. He's clever, yeah, but he's not a weasel. Joe trusts him, and I trust Joe's opinion."

Sara smirked.

"Joe might be too trusting where Tanner is concerned. When we were at the clinic, Tanner and that doctor had a bit of a scene, there's history there. She told me that she was dating Joe, but she seemed very interested in Tanner."

"Laurel is Joe's girl, but what are you saying, you think she and Tanner have a thing going behind Joe's back?"

"I think the potential is there, and if Pullo were out of the picture, they wouldn't even have to sneak around."

Johnny kissed her.

"You have quite an imagination, but here's what I think, I think that you're not ready to let things be, but you'll have to, you gave Tanner your word and you have to keep it. Let the past be, so that the two of us can move forward."

Sara wanted to argue the point, but knew it would be useless, and so she smiled at Johnny and gestured towards the bedroom.

"Weren't we in the middle of something before finding Duke?"

Sara stood and took his hand to lead him towards the bedroom, but Johnny pulled her back onto the sofa and into his arms. After kissing her, he stared into her eyes.

"I think I'm falling in love with you, Sara Blake. What do you think of that?"

Sara's breath caught in her throat, and when she spoke, there was a touch of awe in her voice.

"You're not alone in feeling that way, and I thought that I would never love again."

They kissed once more, before rising as one, and making their way back into the bedroom.

CHAPTER 21 - Just one of the guys

Tanner watched as another cab let out a passenger in front of the Rutherford Hotel.

This man, like the rest of them, was big, looked fit, and carried a suitcase.

For a hotel that was closed for renovation, the Rutherford was doing good business.

The men were mercenaries that Heinz was bringing in to help take over. Not counting the man getting out of the taxi, Tanner had seen four men arrive in the time he'd been watching, and all of them had been greeted at the door by the same man, an old guy wearing an open bathrobe over a pair of faded blue boxer shorts.

The late arrival of the men told Tanner that Heinz ordered them to come as soon as possible, otherwise, why not arrive at an earlier hour and let the old man at the door get his sleep?

Tanner was watching from a roof of a warehouse that sat across the way from the six-story hotel, and was able to hear snatches of conversation. All of the arriving men had spoken German to the man greeting them, all but one that is, and that man was able to speak some German, but conversed better in French, which the old man also spoke.

The hotel was much older than the buildings surrounding it, which were warehouses, and judging by the ornate brickwork and Old-World styling, it was likely built over a hundred years ago.

From his darkened perch across the way, Tanner had a murky view of the lobby, because there was beveled glass set above the entryway doors.

As he watched, the men who had arrived earlier were leaving the hotel together. The new man said something that Tanner couldn't make out, but when one of the other men answered while pointing down the block, Tanner guessed what they were discussing.

It was food, and they were headed to the restaurant on the corner, which was still open.

The new arrival went inside, where he received a keycard for a room from the old man, left his bag by the front desk, and exited the hotel at a run to catch up with his new companions.

Tanner nodded to himself.

A late-night snack sounded like a good idea.

***

Tanner arrived at the restaurant just a few minutes after the others had taken a table.

He wore glasses, had combed his hair differently, wearing it slicked straight back, and had a pack of cigarettes displayed prominently in his shirt pocket. The cigarettes were a German brand named HB, which he had purchased earlier along with the eyeglasses.

The place was quiet, with only a few couples around, other than the table where Heinz's men sat, and they stared at him with interest when he walked in. The men were all clean-shaven, save for one, who had a bushy red mustache.

Tanner called to them in German that had not a trace of an American accent.

"The man in the robe said that you would be here. I just arrived."

One of the men waved him over, and he gave them a name that sounded as phony as theirs did.

Tanner had no doubt that their passports were all fakes, but of good quality. They had come to New York to slaughter other men for money, and they would not be traveling under their true names.

The men talked sports, admired the few women who were about, and drank. Tanner ingratiated himself with the others by buying a round of drinks and being agreeable.

There was also hushed talk about an elite hit squad that was set to arrive in the morning from Brussels.

The other men made derisive comments, and said that they could kill anyone as well as the men coming from Brussels, and that Heinz was just wasting money hiring the so-called elite team of assassins.

When Tanner asked who the men were coming to kill, the man at the table who did most of the talking, the one with the mustache, gave a shrug and said, "Some American asshole who thinks he's Rambo."

By the time they left the restaurant two hours later, the six of them were talking loud and laughing like old friends.

The man in the bathrobe shushed them to be quiet as he let them in, after they'd awakened him again, and Tanner rode up in the only working elevator with the others to the third floor, after taking note that none of the lobby cameras seemed to be working, and that the monitors inside the security office were all dark.

The old man who let them in never gave Tanner a second look, but was just eager to return to bed.

Tanner pretended to swipe a keycard as the others had, and waved goodnight as he grabbed the door handle, but after everyone else had entered their rooms, he went exploring by using the stairs.

He came across Heinz's suite on the top floor, and figured that the rooms were also in use as the man's office. There was an armed thug sitting at a small table outside the door, but he was leaning on an elbow, while reading a magazine.

Tanner debated whether to kill Heinz or wait, and decided to wait and gain information, because he couldn't be certain if the man was inside the suite.

With that decided, he found an unlocked room on the fourth floor. It was a level of the building that the renovation had yet to touch, but that still contained the old furnishings, although the room had a musty odor and the carpet showed stains.

After stacking bottles from the mini fridge in front of the door to act as a makeshift alarm system, Tanner undressed and went to sleep in the belly of the beast.

He was just another hired gun, and to the men he'd met and drank with, just one of the boys.

CHAPTER 22 - Saint Brian

The following morning, after Johnny left to go home and change, Sara agreed to meet her sister for breakfast.

They met in a coffee shop near Sara's apartment. Jennifer had arrived first, and when Sara appeared, Jennifer hugged her.

"I'm sorry about the other day, but I wanted you to know how I feel."

"I think we both spoke our minds," Sara said, as she took a seat.

The two talked about the rest of their family as they ate, with Jennifer filling Sara in on what's been happening.

Jennifer reached across the table and gave her sister's hand a squeeze.

"I'm so glad that we've made up before I left on my trip. I have to fly down to Guambi tonight and I may not be back for weeks. The charity is setting up an aide center to help the victims of the typhoon they had."

Sara looked concerned.

"Couldn't you send someone else, it's dangerous there."

"I run the charity, and the danger is minimal. I learned yesterday that President Urray, the new leader, has firmly taken control of the government, and there are elections planned for later this year."

"What about Jake?"

"What do you mean?"

"Do you really trust him enough to be separated for weeks? And don't give me that look, I know the man, and it's asking a lot for him to be celibate while you're gone."

Jennifer's mouth opened in shock.

"That, that is so rude. I trust Jake, and unlike Johnny Rossetti, he doesn't work in an environment where naked women are the norm, and God only knows what goes on inside that club."

"Those women are dancers, performers, not hookers, and maybe you shouldn't judge them without knowing them."

Jennifer took a deep breath, held it for a moment, and let it out slowly.

"You're right, I shouldn't judge or jump to conclusions, but you shouldn't be so quick to judge Jake either, he's changed, Sara. He nearly died thanks to you, and it changed him."

Sara narrowed her eyes.

"He's holding a grudge against me, isn't he?"

"Jake? No, he likes you."

"Maybe not, and maybe he's with you as a way to pay me back."

"Sara, Jake and I being together has nothing to do with you, and I find it insulting that you would think so."

"Oh, honey no, I know he's attracted to you, any man would be, but he knew that I didn't want him to date you, and he went after you anyway. That makes me even more afraid that he's planning on breaking your heart, as a way of getting back at me."

Jennifer grabbed a napkin from the table and wiped at her eyes.

"I'm going to leave before I say something I'll regret."

"I didn't mean to hurt you, Jenny, and someday you'll see that I'm right about Jake."

"Because I couldn't possibly be enough for him, right?"

"Oh, Jenny, no, it's not about you, I just think that—"

Jennifer stood, rummaged in her purse, and when her hand came out, it was holding money. She tossed the bills atop the table and stared at her sister.

"I'll call you when I get back from my trip."

"Jenny? Don't be mad. I just know Jake better than you do."

Jennifer shook her head slightly, started to walk away, but then turned back.

"You've built your life around this insane quest to get revenge for Brian's death, but let me tell you something, the man was no saint."

Sara jerked in her seat, shocked by the vehemence in her sister's voice.

"What are you saying?"

"The Fourth of July party, remember? Brian gave me a lift home."

"Yes, so?"

"After I opened the door of my apartment, he made a pass at me."

"That's a lie!"

"No, it's the God's honest truth. He kissed me, and after I pushed him away, he apologized. When I told him that I thought he'd had too much to drink, he agreed to take a cab to your place and left his car."

"I remember him taking a cab, but he said he had car trouble."

"No, he had trouble keeping his hands to himself."

"You must have misunderstood. He was, he was just being friendly."

"Of course, Saint Brian would never do anything wrong."

Sara's face reddened with anger.

"Don't talk about him like that, and what is this? Are you saying that I don't have a right to seek justice?"

"You could have had justice in Las Vegas if you had simply done your job. That man Tanner would be rotting away in a prison right this minute, but no, your bloodlust had to be satisfied, and it nearly cost Jake his life."

"You don't understand, Jenny, but that's no reason to make up lies about Brian."

"I'm not lying. The man practically stuck his tongue down my throat."

Sara stood, and the chair she was in made a scraping sound that caused the coffee shop's other patrons to look their way.

"Brian loved me. I know he did."

Jennifer nodded.

"I think so too, it's why I accepted his apology for kissing me and chalked it up to too much alcohol, and, it's also why I never said anything to you."

Sara stared down at the floor.

"It didn't happen, you must have misunderstood."

"It's the truth."

"Liar," Sara said, but there was no force behind the word.

Jennifer sighed.

"Goodbye Sara,"

After Jennifer walked out, Sara sank back down into her chair, took out her phone, and gazed at a photo of Brian Ames.

CHAPTER 23 - Dead men driving

Tanner wiped down the room he had slept in, obliterating his prints, and went downstairs to the hotel's dining room, where several of the men from the night before were gathered at one end of a long table.

It was mid-morning, and the word was going around that the hit team from Brussels would be arriving soon.

There were no servants in the hotel, but Heinz had given some of his people the tasks of working as such, and Tanner watched as one man rolled a cart of coffee and pastries onto the elevator.

The food was going up to the top floor. Heinz's suite was up there, but there was a second suite of rooms, and also a conference room for meetings.

When the four-man hit team arrived with Heinz, Tanner realized that he had glimpsed the bald German before. It was the day he had killed Frank Richards, and Heinz was one of the men trapped in the room with the automatic gun.

Now, Heinz was looking to take Richards' place, and the four men with him were hired to help make that wish a reality.

All four men looked fit, were Caucasian, and were already armed, judging by the bulge of holsters beneath the jackets they each wore.

The jackets were made of black leather, and had a distinct design on their backs in white, and also a smaller version of the same illustration over the front breast pocket in red. It took Tanner a few moments to realize what the design was, and when he did, he nearly rolled his eyes.

It was the Chinese symbol for death.

The biggest of the men was well over six feet tall and had a shaved head, while the smallest was two or three inches shorter than Tanner was, and wore his long dark hair tied back in a ponytail.

The other two men were Tanner's height and sported buzz cuts, one blond, one dark, although the blond one also wore a black baseball cap with the words, *Deutscher Fussball Bund*, which translated to, German Football Association. Apparently, the man was a soccer fan.

Heinz looked over the assembled crowd, which Tanner had counted as being twenty-five men, and the bald German showed no glint of recognition, as his eyes passed over Tanner in his glasses and slicked back hair. This, despite the fact that Heinz was holding a picture of Tanner aloft for all to see,

It was the mugshot of Tanner taken earlier in the year by Mexican authorities, and the only thing exceptional about the face in the photo were the eyes, which burned with rage at having been betrayed and captured.

Heinz spoke while moving the photo from side to side, so that everyone in the room could get a look.

"This is a photo of an American assassin named Tanner. These four men are here to see that today is his last. Once they succeed, we will move forward with our plans."

Tanner looked around without being obvious about it, and saw that no one was staring at him. The last place they expected the man in the photo to be was standing at their side.

Heinz continued.

"The Americans, these Mafia toughs, they are afraid of this man, and he has killed them with ease, but these four men here will show them what real killers are, and together we will take this city right out of their hands."

There were nods and grunts of agreement, and one man even clapped, but stopped as Heinz glared at him. He then removed a stack of the same photo from an envelope, and instructed one of his people to pass them around.

When Tanner received his, he made a sound of derision after reading the height and weight listed.

"This man is no bigger than me, and I thought he would be a giant."

The Frenchman who spoke little German agreed. He was a large man, and declared that he could kill Tanner with one hand.

Tanner slipped away before the hit team boarded the elevator with Heinz, and made his way to the stairwell, where he ran up the six flights without stopping until he reached the top.

The conference room was across from the stairway door, and Tanner could see through the mesh glass set in the metal door that the men hadn't entered the room yet. However, when he eased the door open, he heard the elevator chime its arrival.

Tanner slipped into the hall and entered the men's room near the end of the corridor, which sat across and to the right of the conference room.

Heinz stepped off the elevator while talking to the hit team. He was informing them that he had a call to make, and that he would be joining them shortly in the conference room.

After putting down the toilet seat inside one of the stalls, Tanner sat atop the toilet tank and waited for his prey to come to him, like a spider waiting inside a web.

***

At the rear of the Cabaret Strip Club, Merle and Earl stayed busy by polishing the limo with rags, while they waited for Joe Pullo to appear.

They had gotten a call earlier to meet Pullo at the club, and both brothers were anxious, and wondered about the purpose of the meeting.

However, of the two of them, Earl was by far the most nervous.

"I'm telling you, he's coming to kill us."

Merle shook his head in disagreement.

"No he ain't. Why would he kill us now? If they were gonna kill us, they'd have done it already."

"Okay, then why does he want to see us?"

"I don't know, maybe he wants us to do something, and that's good. If we run a few errands and do things for him, then maybe Pullo will start to like us."

Earl frowned.

"I don't care if he ever likes me; I just don't want him to kill me."

The sound of an engine came from the front of the building, where the other gate was. The alley curved, but they could tell it was a large engine, and when they heard the sound of the other gate being unlocked, they knew that Pullo had arrived in his Hummer.

Their assumption was confirmed just moments later, when after driving in and relocking the gate, Pullo drove around the bend and parked by the rear door that led to the office.

Merle and Earl watched as Pullo exited his vehicle and walked towards them with purposeful strides.

"Good morning, Mr. Pullo," the boys said in stereo, and were greeted with only silence.

Pullo shifted his eyes towards the rear of the limo, and Merle rushed over and opened the door for him.

"You want us to take you somewhere?" Earl asked.

Pullo nodded.

"Yeah boys, you and I are going for a little ride."

Earl looked over at his brother, and by the look on his face, he saw that Merle finally got it. They were dead men.

CHAPTER 24 - Bathroom break

The first of the hit team members entered the bathroom.

It was the blond man with the buzz cut and baseball cap.

Through the crack in the stall door, Tanner could spot the man's back in the mirror, as he lined himself up with one of the urinals.

The bathroom contained three urinals on the left, with a line of four stalls to their right, and across from the stalls were a row of sinks, with a long mirror above them, and on the wall beside that, was a hot air machine for use in drying hands.

From his perch inside the second stall, Tanner heard the sound of the man's zipper going down, followed by the splash of liquid against porcelain.

That was when Tanner struck, as he came up silently behind the man and plunged the blade of his knife deep into the back of the man's skull, directly beneath the adjustable strap at the rear of the ball cap.

The man grunted in shock as his mouth opened in surprise, and then he fell to the floor with a severe spinal injury, but was still alive. Tanner remedied the latter condition by smashing the lid from a commode atop the man's head, which cracked his skull open.

After dragging the man's body into the last stall and propping him in the corner, Tanner used the man's shirt to clean up the spilled blood and piss, and was standing at the same urinal when the next man walked in.

Tanner wasn't blond, wore boots instead of the bright sneakers worn by the man he had just killed, and was also wearing suit pants and not jeans, but between the black leather jacket and the baseball cap he wore, he fooled the next man long enough to kill him, as the man sidled up to the urinal beside him.

It was the largest of the men, the one with the shaved head.

Tanner jammed a boot heel into the back of the man's knee, causing him to fall forward and bang his face against the steel flush valve atop the urinal, which broke several of the man's front teeth, and caused him to stumble backwards and fall to his knees.

The man spit out the pieces of his broken teeth, but the pain in the man's mouth became a secondary consideration when Tanner reached around and sliced the man's throat open.

The blood left the man's body with such force that it painted the mirrors above the sinks red, and filled the room with its coppery scent.

Tanner let the man drop, stepped out in the hallway, and came face-to-face with another member of the hit team, the man with the dark crew cut.

The man had been headed into the bathroom while talking on the phone, and Tanner shot him twice in the face, with one bullet entering his open mouth.

He then followed the man to the floor, to lay half in and half out of the bathroom, with his face turned away, and the gun tucked out of sight.

"Hans!" the last man cried out, the one with the ponytail, as he sprinted from the conference room in reaction to hearing the shots, and Tanner heard his footfalls grow closer.

The man cursed loudly in Dutch when he saw his friend's body, and Tanner felt a gentle hand touch his shoulder.

"Seth, where is the shooter?"

"I'm right here," Tanner said, while turning over and shooting the man three times in the stomach.

The man fell backwards to the carpet, dying, and soon to be dead. Tanner claimed his gun, a Beretta FS92, and took aim at Bruno Heinz, who was standing in the doorway of the conference room with eyes made large from astonishment.

"Tanner?"

Tanner fired an instant after Heinz was yanked backwards into the conference room, and his shot passed through the doorway and struck a picture on the wall.

"Tanner! Is that you?"

Tanner thought the voice sounded familiar, but couldn't place it.

"My name is Vance, Tanner, and unlike those four fools with the matching jackets, I'm man enough to kill you, and I'm going to do just that."

Tanner could hear Heinz yelling into a phone. That meant that more men would be coming.

He had to get by the conference room to access either the stairway or the elevators, which meant he had to get past Vance.

Johnny Rossetti was paying him a small fortune to take down Heinz, and Tanner realized that he was going to have to earn every cent of it.

CHAPTER 25 - Cold sweat

Merle's hands were gripped tightly upon the steering wheel of the limo, as he and Earl headed for the George Washington Bridge.

Pullo had yet to tell them their destination, but simply said to take the bridge into New Jersey, a state where the Giacconi Family liked to dump their bodies.

Pullo had instructed the boys to leave the partition open while they drove, and so the two brothers couldn't talk freely, but each one knew by the other's expression that they were both fearful.

Earl shook his head slightly as he thought of Tanner, and cursed the day that he and Merle had met the man. They had been threatened with death several times since entering Tanner's orbit, and it looked like their luck was about to run out.

"Damn Tanner," he muttered.

Merle had heard the whispered curse, and nodded his head in agreement.

***

Pullo sat in the rear of the limo in a somber mood.

While he was angry that the Carter brothers hadn't told them that Tanner was alive when they believed he was dead, he held no real animosity towards the men.

Killing them was a precautionary measure, nothing more and nothing less, and he would take no pleasure in the act.

His phone rang. It was Laurel.

"What's up, Beautiful?"

"Can you come by the clinic? I need to see you."

"Right now, or can it wait a few hours?"

"Now would be better, why, are you out of the area?"

"No, but I was headed into Jersey, but hold on a second."

Pullo covered the phone with his hand and spoke to Merle.

"We have to make a detour, boys, turn around and head to West 26th and Tenth Avenue."

Merle acknowledged the request with an accompanying sigh of relief, and Pullo spoke to Laurel again.

"I'll be there soon, but what's up?"

"I'd rather tell you in person, but don't worry, it's not serious."

"Okay," Pullo said, while not liking the note of dread he heard in her voice, but he decided to push it aside and not dwell on it.

He and Laurel spoke for another minute, before ending the call.

"Hey you two?"

Merle looked at Pullo in the mirror, while Earl turned around in his seat.

"Yes sir," the boys said together.

"You don't have wives or girlfriends, do you?"

"No, women only seem to like us in small doses," Earl said.

Pullo laughed.

"You're lucky; they're a lot of work sometimes,"

Merle caught Pullo's eye in the mirror.

"Are we really lucky?"

The humor left Pullo's face.

"No, maybe not,"

And the way Pullo said it, made both brothers break out in a cold sweat.

CHAPTER 26 - The best

Tanner dragged the man with the ponytail into the bathroom and checked to see if he was dead yet. He was, and Tanner went to work cutting off the ponytail.

With that done, he set a roll of toilet paper on fire and held it up to the sprinkler head in the ceiling, and hoped that the renovation hadn't disabled the fire control system.

The system was still functional, and within seconds, the sprinkler activated, showering him with water, but more importantly, it triggered the fire alarm, and with the fire alarm operative, the safety controls in the elevator would refuse to send the car up to the floor, and would let out all passengers onto lower floors.

With the reinforcements delayed, Tanner exited the bathroom while firing towards the conference room.

Vance had ventured out into the hall, and Tanner's bold advance surprised him, and caused him to dive back into the conference room.

Tanner kept coming, he had little leeway for doing anything else, or he risked being trapped.

Vance fired at him as he opened the door to the stairway, and Tanner cried out in pain as a bullet sliced open his side, just beneath the left ribs.

The pain of the wound weakened him, and after rushing into the stairwell, he nearly tumbled down the steps, but caught hold of the railing just in time to halt his momentum.

He was on the landing when the door opened, and he fired a shot that drove Vance back beyond the door.

Tanner headed down the stairs, and was on the landing between the fourth and fifth floors when he heard Vance enter the stairwell again, and when the door opened and three men with guns entered from the fourth floor hallway, Tanner pointed up.

"The man named Vance has gone mad, kill him!"

The men looked at him. He was still wearing the black leather jacket of the hit team along with the baseball cap, and hanging down his back was a ponytail. After cutting it off the dead man in the bathroom, Tanner had tied it to the rear of the cap.

Everything about him said hit team member, and so the men ran past him and headed up the stairs. When they ran into Vance, a firefight ensued.

Tanner kept moving, his one objective was now aimed at escaping, and when he reached the door that led to the second floor, he leaned against it, resting for a just a moment, as the wound in his side sapped his strength and turned the white shirt beneath the jacket blood red.

"Tanner!"

It was Vance. He had won the firefight against the three men in an impressively short space of time and was back on his trail.

From the sound of his voice, Vance was still two flights away, but Tanner knew that translated to a very narrow gap of time.

He found no one on the second floor and ran towards the rear of the building. At the end of the hall was a large window, and Tanner fired at the glass before he reached it.

With the glass gone, he stepped up onto the windowsill, bent his knees, and jumped, to land atop the dumpster in the back.

He was in his car and driving away when he spotted Vance in his rear view mirror, as the man left the alley and ran into the street.

Vance stomped his foot in frustration while keeping his gun hidden, not daring to risk taking a shot, as several other cars and pedestrians were about.

The last glimpse Tanner had of the man, he saw that he was pointing in his direction, in essence saying, there will be a next time.

Tanner agreed, but next time, only one of them would be walking away.

***

Pullo stepped out of the limo in front of Laurel's clinic and Merle and Earl gave him a puzzled look. The clinic was located in the rear of a squat building surrounded by a high fence that had an antiques shop in the front, and its entrance, an old rusty metal door, sat below a tattered green awning.

"Are you buying antiques, Boss?"

"No, now stay with the limo and I'll be back in a few minutes."

Merle and Earl watched as Pullo input a code into a control pad near the door and entered the building.

With Pullo out of sight, both men breathed a sigh of relief.

"You still think he don't want to kill us?" Earl said.

"I don't know. For a while there I thought that was where we were heading, but if that was true, why leave us alone?"

Earl thought about that, and became confused, after being certain that Pullo wanted them dead.

"Damn! I like this job. Rossetti treats us right, and we get to wear suits, look at hot women, and don't have to work hard."

"What? Are you starting to think that Pullo doesn't want us dead?"

"I don't know, but I get the willies every time he looks at me."

Merle scratched his head, as he tried to figure out what to do.

"If we run, and they don't want to kill us, then, they might start thinking that we did something and send somebody to kill us."

Earl slapped the dashboard.

"Why can't life be simple?"

"It is simple. If they want to kill us, we'll be dead soon, if not, we keep this sweet job, but simple don't make it easy."

"What do we do, Merle?"

Merle looked over at his brother.

"I'm thinking."

Earl leaned back in his seat. When Merle thought about something, it could take a long time.

***

Inside the clinic, Laurel separated from Pullo after sharing a kiss, and took the piece of paper from her pocket that Tanner had given her.

"What's that?" Pullo said.

"Tanner gave it to me last night at the house."

Pullo's expression hardened.

"He came by to see you, and what happened?"

"Nothing, I swear, and I don't think he was expecting anything to either, but he gave me this number where I could reach him. He said that the Giacconi Family was going to war, and he wanted me to be able to reach him in case I needed him... needed him in case of trouble."

Pullo looked down at the paper and then back into Laurel's eyes.

"Did you want something to happen? I know you still love him."

Laurel hugged Pullo.

"Tanner is a part of my past. I'm with you now, and the reason I'm telling you about this is, well, I don't want any secrets between us."

Pullo tilted her head back and stared into her eyes.

"I care about you, Laurel. These last few weeks, they've been the best of my life."

Laurel smiled.

"We're just getting started."

They kissed again, and when they separated, Pullo pointed at the number Tanner had given her.

"Keep that. Tanner was right, there's trouble coming, and if it comes here, between the two of us, we'll stop it."

Laurel smiled.

"No one would attack the clinic. We're like the Red Cross."

Pullo took her by the hand and began walking towards the door.

"I have to get going, but I'll be back in town in time for dinner, so why don't we go out?"

"That sounds great, but where do you want to go?"

"Anywhere is good for me, baby, as long as I'm with you."

Pullo opened the door and stepped outside. The first thing he saw was the empty limo, but then he spotted Merle and Earl. They were at the rear of the vehicle and headed for the fence.

Merle had finished his deep thinking just seconds ago, and had concluded that they should run and hide.

"Hey! Where are you two going?"

The boys spun around and Pullo saw the fear in their eyes, but then, something bizarre occurred, as first Earl, and then Merle, gawked at him, and began pointing his way.

The two brothers then turned and stared at each other, as if to verify that they were seeing the same thing, and yes, both of them had the same wondrous look in their eyes, and when they turned back around, there were tears forming, even as their faces wore wide grins.

What the hell? Pullo thought, as he took in the spectacle, but no sooner had he pondered the boys' strange reaction, when Laurel rushed past him and ran towards the brothers with open arms, and she was shouting their names.

"Merle! Earl!"

The brothers also opened their arms to receive her, and Laurel hugged first one, and then the other, before the three of them came together in a tangle of arms, while tears of joy rolled down their faces, as Merle and Earl kept asking the same question over and over.

"Laurel Lee, oh Laurel Lee, is it really you?"

Pullo broke from his trance and walked over to join them.

"What the hell is going on here?"

Laurel wrapped an arm around each of the boy's waists, and smiled at Pullo, as pure happiness radiated in her eyes.

"Joe, this is Merle and Earl. They're my big brothers."

Pullo stared at the three of them, as a horrified look animated his features.

"What? No, that's not possible."

Laurel kissed the boys on the cheek.

"We had the same daddy, and now that we've found each other after so many years, we'll never be separated again. Isn't it just the best?"

Pullo stared at the boys' grinning faces.

"Yeah, the best,"

CHAPTER 27 - *Thumpity, Thumpity, Thump,*

As he drove towards Midtown, Tanner took out his phone and called Sophia.

"Where you at, baby?" she said.

"I've been shot. The wound is bleeding badly, but I don't think it's serious because the bullet just nicked me. Does the Calvino Family have any clinics in the city?"

"No, ours are only on Staten Island, but there's one we use on West 26th, or somewhere around there, and I heard that the doctor is good. Go there, and are you sure it's not bad?"

"I'm sure, and yeah, I'll go there."

"I'll meet you after I change and shower, and be careful."

"Sophia," Tanner said, but she had already hung up.

He had wanted to avoid seeing Laurel again, but it looked like it couldn't be helped, as the wound on his side definitely needed attention.

He saw her face in his mind's eye, and the hint of a smile curled his lips.

***

Inside Laurel Ivy's clinic, Pullo learned about the branches of the Carter Family tree.

"My mama married Merle and Earl's daddy, my daddy, a few years after the boys' mama died," Laurel said, and Pullo noticed that her slight southern accent had deepened.

Merle took over the story.

"Daddy died when Laurel Lee was just a little thing, and then she and her mama moved north."

"I wasn't that young," Laurel said. "I was twelve, but small for my age, and after we moved here, to Brooklyn actually, Mama married a man named Bruce Ivy, and he became my new daddy, and later, I took his name."

Pullo looked at the homely Merle and Earl and then at the walking dream that was Laurel.

"You must look just like your mother, honey, because there's not a scrap of them in you."

Laurel kissed her brothers on the cheek again.

"These two spoiled me rotten as I was growing up, and I've been searching for them for years. I even went back to Arkansas once to look for them."

"We used to move around a lot," Earl said. "But we're firmly planted now that Mr. Rossetti has made us his chauffeurs."

Not as firmly planted as you would have been had we not stopped here, Pullo thought, but every time he saw the joy in Laurel's eyes, he couldn't help but be glad that the three of them had reunited.

"I'll take a taxi back to the club, and you boys can stay here with Laurel and catch up. Take the rest of the day off, but you still need to pick Johnny up at the club tonight."

Merle grinned.

"Thanks Mr. Pullo."

"Mr. Pullo? No, call him Joe," Laurel said. "I want you three to become good friends."

"Can we really call you Joe?" Earl asked.

Pullo forced a smile.

"Whatever Laurel wants is fine by me."

***

Tanner pulled up outside the gate while Pullo was waiting for his taxi.

Pullo winced after Tanner stepped out of the car, opened the jacket, and showed him his wound.

"That's nasty, but you're lucky the round didn't hit a rib, and why are your clothes damp?"

"That's a long story, but you can let Rossetti know that Heinz has fewer men today than he did yesterday."

"Where are they?"

"Uptown, the Rutherford Hotel on Randall Street,"

"How many men does he have?"

"At last count, twenty-two, mostly Mercs from Europe, and one more thing, Vance is with them."

"The Russian? Johnny will be interested in hearing that."

As Pullo's taxi arrived, Tanner pointed towards the clinic door.

"I think I'll get sewn up now."

Pullo grabbed his arm and halted him before he could take a step.

"Laurel told me about your late-night visit."

"Then you also know why I was there, to give her that number."

"You could have done that on the phone. I'm not a fool, Tanner. If you want Laurel, just come out and say it, and, if she chooses you, well, alright then, but I just want her to be happy."

"She's happy with you, Joe, and I wasn't there to make a move. If I had, she would have shown me the door. I had my chance with Laurel, and I walked away."

Pullo let go of his arm.

"That makes you a fool."

"No, it leaves me free."

***

Tanner was greeted by the sight of Merle, Earl, and Laurel holding hands, after she buzzed him inside the clinic, and like Pullo, he was amazed.

"I remember you telling me about your big brothers, but I never would have imagined it was these two."

Laurel saw the way the three men were looking at each other, and realized that they weren't strangers.

"You three know each other, for how long?"

"Oh, the boys and I have had a few adventures together, isn't that right boys?"

Merle looked back and forth between his sister and Tanner.

"You two are friends?"

Tanner smiled at Laurel.

"I like to think so."

Laurel turned and walked towards a treatment room.

"You boys wait out here while I treat Tanner, and then we'll go have an early lunch and catch-up."

Tanner followed her into a small room and sat atop an examining table. Laurel grimaced with concern when she saw the wound on his left side.

"You'll need stitches."

"I figured that,"

Her eyes took in the rest of his bare torso, and a frown of concern clouded her face.

"So many new scars, why do you live so dangerously?"

Tanner gazed into her eyes, and once again, his heart rate escalated.

Thumpity, Thumpity, Thump, his heart went,

He had been intimate with women who affected him less than Laurel did with just a glance.

"There are greater dangers than the ones I face," Tanner said.

Laurel stitched him up, and as she was applying the bandage to his side, she paused and gazed at him.

Tanner stared back at her, and became lost in her eyes, as the moment stretched on, and their lips grew closer.

"I see you're in good hands," said a voice from the doorway, and when Tanner looked over, he saw Sophia staring at them.

Laurel cleared her throat.

"Who are you?"

"She's Sophia Verona, she's with me," Tanner said.

Sophia tossed a thumb over her shoulder.

"Johnny's chauffeurs let me in, they know me."

When Laurel finished treating Tanner's wound, Sophia walked over and kissed him, and then she looked at Laurel for a reaction, and saw that the doctor's demeanor had grown colder, as she returned her stare.

Laurel then looked away from Sophia and back at Tanner.

"Um, I'll give you something for the pain, and you'll need to take it easy, or those stitches might tear. I also want you to change that bandage daily."

"I'll take care of that," Sophia said.

Laurel looked at Tanner.

"You two are living together?"

"It's temporary," Tanner said, and Sophia gave him a look that said that was news to her.

Once outside the clinic and in the car, Sophia gazed at Tanner expectantly. She was behind the wheel, so that Tanner could rest.

When he realized that she was staring at him instead of starting the car, he looked back at her.

"What?"

"Don't give me that, 'What?', you and the doc, you had a thing going once, didn't you?"

"Yes, but it was years ago,"

"Gone but not forgotten, judging by the scene I saw when I walked in on you, if I had arrived a minute later, you two would have been going at it on top of that treatment table."

"Laurel is Joe Pullo's girl."

"Damn Tanner, Pullo will shoot you if you touch her… and so would I."

Tanner sighed.

"I think it's time we separated."

"Why? You think I'm clingy, well I'm not. I just like you, in and out of bed. So shut up, you're stuck with me for now, and you're coming back to the hotel and rest up, and I'll also order some food from room service."

Tanner smiled.

"Yes ma'am, whatever you say."

"Damn straight," Sophia said, and then she started the car and drove away from the clinic.

CHAPTER 28 - Too clever by half

Sara was tracking Tanner's movements and growing suspicious.

She had gone to Laurel's townhouse earlier, after being led there by following Tanner's trail, and after doing a search on the property's title, she discovered that Laurel owned it.

She assumed it meant that Tanner was sleeping with Laurel behind Pullo's back, and was further proof that the man couldn't be trusted.

The tracker data also told her that Tanner had spent the night at the Rutherford Hotel on Randall Street, and when she drove by the building, she saw that it was closed for renovation and not accepting guests.

After turning around, she found a place to park in front of a fire hydrant, and after twenty minutes of observation, she could tell that something was going on at the Rutherford, and that rather than being empty of guests, it was a hive of activity.

She phoned Johnny Rossetti at the club and played a hunch.

"This man Heinz who wants to take Frank Richards place as leader of The Conglomerate, do you know where he is?"

"Yeah, Joe just called. Heinz is using a hotel as his base, and Tanner already had another battle with his men there."

"Tanner told you that he killed some of Heinz's men?"

"Yeah, and he was wounded too, but not seriously."

"Too bad they didn't kill him, but are you certain he was really injured?"

"Yeah, Joe saw the wound himself. Sara, what's going on? You gave the man your word that you wouldn't try to kill him."

"Nothing's going on, and I'll call again later, stay safe, bye bye,"

After hanging up, Sara nibbled her bottom lip. According to the tracker, Tanner stayed at the hotel all night.

That sounds like something a guest would do, not an attacker,

Tanner was planning a double-cross. Sara was certain of it, but she would need proof before she could act on the information or convince Johnny, but she was determined to beat Tanner.

She smiled.

Tanner had made sure that Pullo could attest that he was wounded, which gave credence to his statement that he'd been in battle against Heinz.

You smart, tricky bastard,

Sara hated Tanner with a passion, but a part of her admired the man as well. He was devilishly cunning, and had survived many times because of it. That, and his ruthlessness and skill at killing,

You won't win this time Tanner. This time, you'll be outsmarted.

Sara refreshed the tracker info, and recognized the address that Tanner had recently visited. It was Laurel's clinic. Tanner's wound—a wound that Sara had no doubts was self-inflicted—had not only been useful in convincing Johnny that Tanner was on his side, but also gave the assassin an excuse to visit his lover.

"Tricky, tricky, Tanner,"

Sara started her car, and headed off to see Laurel Ivy.

CHAPTER 29 - Obsession

Inside the Rutherford Hotel, Bruno Heinz looked on in disgust, as the bodies of his vaunted hit team were loaded onto the elevator to be taken away and buried in unmarked graves.

There were more bodies in the stairwell, but those three were killed by Vance after Tanner had tricked them into thinking he was the enemy, while he made his escape.

Heinz was scarlet with rage, but he forced himself to remain silent and tried to think of his next move.

After downing a drink, he settled at the conference room table and looked across at Vance.

"Do you have any suggestions?"

"I do, but first, a question."

"Go ahead,"

"As part of The Conglomerate, you have inside knowledge about Rossetti's operations, yes?"

"That's true, your point."

"I think you should acquire more men, attack them all at the same time, and simply overwhelm them with a superior force. Rossetti's own war with Tanner has left his troop levels low, and the men that remain aren't the best. With enough men, you could take over his territory in one night."

Heinz shook his head sadly.

"I don't have nearly enough men for that, and bringing in more is always problematic."

"That's true, but you're thinking about imported men from Europe, but what I'm talking about is a simple show of force, and if I wanted to, I could have hundreds of local street soldiers here in a day. Of course, it would mean sharing power, but in one night, New York would be yours."

"How could you possibly acquire hundreds of men in one day?"

"Michael Krupin, Mikhail Krupin's son, with his father disabled by a stroke, he now leads the Russian gangs in New York, and he is willing to join forces with you in order to take over Rossetti's territory."

Heinz stood, walked over to the window, but then thought about Tanner, and closed the drapes.

"Your plan sounds feasible, but there is no way that I will give up my power, and even if I was willing to join forces with this Russian, it would all be for nothing if Rossetti attacks before we're ready."

Vance smiled.

"I can make sure that Rossetti holds off on taking further action by pretending to want to make a deal."

"A meeting? You would risk that?"

"I would, it would also give me a chance to see Tanner up close."

"You want the pleasure of killing him, don't you?"

"The man is the best, and once I kill him, that title will be mine. As disastrous as it was for you, his killing of the hit team was masterful. He killed the men one by one as they were discussing how to track him down. He's completely unconventional, and I'll have to be just as unorthodox to beat him."

"How so?"

"I don't know yet, but I won't come at him head on. He's too good for that."

"A meeting to delay things might work; however, I've already set in motion a new plan. If it's unsuccessful, then we'll try your approach."

"What plan?"

Heinz smiled.

"The old-fashioned kind, and Rossetti won't see it coming."

***

Inside his office at the club, Johnny offered his hand to Jade Taylor, and studied the woman as they shook hands. Pullo had told him that she was not only beautiful, but exotic, and Johnny had to agree.

"Before you tell me why you're here, Agent Taylor, let me first offer condolences on the death of your friend, Agent Geary."

Jade Taylor blinked in surprise.

"Thank you, Mr. Rossetti, that was unexpectedly civilized of you."

"I have my moments," Johnny said, and then the two of them settled in their seats, on opposite sides of his desk.

The new doors had been installed, and while the rear door only offered a tinted view of the alley behind the building, the door leading to the hallway gave a partial view of the bar area.

"I'm certain that Mr. Pullo told you my intent."

"He did, and I'll tell you right now that you're wasting your time. I've had six audits in the past seven years, and three of those times, it was discovered that I had overpaid my taxes. I run a legitimate business here, and that's the truth."

Jade laughed, the sound was musical, and reverberated within the small office.

"You make millions in illegal income and we both know it, so don't play innocent, and know this, I'm a very patient woman, and no matter how long it takes, I'll nail you."

Johnny stood.

"I guess there's nothing else to say."

Jade headed for the door.

"I'll show myself out, but I'll be back."

Johnny watched her as she headed down the hallway, and saw her acknowledge Pullo with a nod as she passed him near the bar.

When Pullo entered the office, Johnny checked his watch.

"That was quick, what did you do, dump the Carter brothers in the East River?"

Pullo sat in the chair recently occupied by Jade Taylor, and let out a long breath.

"You're not going to believe this."

***

By the time Pullo was finished telling him the story of Merle and Earl's reunion with Laurel, Johnny was laughing.

"If you kill them it will break Laurel's heart, and if she ever found out that you were the one who pulled the trigger, she'd—"

"I know. It's why they're still breathing."

"You know what this means, right?"

"What?"

"Those two are now your responsibility. If they screw up, I'll hold you partly to blame."

Pullo sat up straight.

"How do you figure that?"

"You're the one who said that they were a threat and that they needed to go. What's changed? I mean, other than the fact that they're Laurel's brothers,"

Pullo thought that over and cursed.

"If only we hadn't stopped at the clinic."

"Don't sweat it, the boys aren't the brightest bulbs you'll find, but they're not greedy or looking to cause trouble either. They'll be fine."

Pullo smiled.

"They made Laurel happy; I never saw her smile so wide."

"Good, now what about Tanner, you said on the phone that he wasn't hurt badly?"

"A bullet creased his ribs, but he's tough."

Johnny smiled, and then laughed again.

"What's funny now?"

"I was just thinking, if you and Laurel ever marry, then you, Merle, and Earl would be family."

"That's what I get for not dating an Italian girl."

***

Laurel looked at the monitor that was connected to the camera, which was pointed at the gate, and saw Sara staring back at her. When she let her inside the clinic, she was surprised to learn that Merle and Earl also knew Sara.

"Oh, but I guess they met you through Johnny?"

"No, I first met Merle and Earl in Las Vegas, but that's a long story."

Merle smiled at Sara.

"She arrested me once, back when she was a Fed, but the charge was dropped, and did ya'll know that the Vegas jail has really good food?"

Laurel looked pained.

"No, but you'll have to tell me all about it sometime."

Laurel and Sara talked in a treatment room while the boys were busy hitting on her nurse, Maya, and asking her if she had a sister.

"What brings you here?" Laurel asked Sara.

"I'll just come out and say it. I know that you and Tanner are sleeping around behind Joe Pullo's back, but what I need to know is, how serious is it?"

Laurel's mouth dropped open.

"Tanner and I... that's... nothing is happening between us, and even if there were an intimate relationship, what business would it be of yours?"

"I saw you two the other day, and that didn't appear to be nothing. Tanner doesn't love you, but he cares about you, doesn't he?"

Laurel looked as if someone had punched her, as she bent over slightly, and her eyes became moist.

"Why do you say he doesn't love me? Is it that obvious?"

Sara's mouth dropped open as the truth hit her.

"You love him. You're in love with Tanner?"

Laurel wiped her tears away.

"Nothing is going on between us, not now, but at one time, we were close, at least I thought so."

"When I said Tanner didn't love you, I meant that he didn't love anyone. He's not capable of it."

"What?"

"The man is a sociopath. It's not possible for him to have feelings."

"No, Tanner, he's... he's imperturbable? Yes, but he's not heartless."

"I think Tanner wants you, and I think he's willing to kill for you. If you have any feelings for Joe Pullo, you might want to break things off with Tanner before he decides that Joe is in the way."

"You're crazy! Tanner would never hurt Joe, they're friends, and I told you, I'm not sleeping with Tanner."

Sara gathered her purse and stood.

"You've been warned."

Laurel walked Sara to the door, and as she watched the former FBI agent stride back to her car, she wondered just what it was about Tanner that obsessed the woman so much.

CHAPTER 30 - Rampage

The last of the patrons left the Cabaret Strip Club with bellies full of overpriced beer and minds brimming with unfulfilled fantasies.

Pullo had left hours earlier, and after Carl the bartender said goodnight along with most of the staff, the head bouncer, Bull, was the only man left with Johnny. The office door was open, and Bull stuck his head in.

"The Carter brothers are here with the limo. They're in the alley."

"Good, and is everything locked up out front?"

"Yeah, so why don't we go out the back way here?"

Johnny agreed, and after turning out the lights, he opened the rear door of the office and stepped into the alley.

When he didn't see the limo, he turned to look at Bull, and saw that he was pointing a gun at him.

"What the fuck, Bull?"

Bull shrugged.

"Sorry Johnny, I really am, but Heinz is paying me a fortune for this, and it's enough to open my own club."

"You scumbag! You sold me out for a few dollars?"

"No, I sold you out for a shitload of dollars. Now close your eyes and I'll make this quick."

Headlights brightened the alleyway, as the limo entered from the street. Johnny tried to take Bull's gun away, but the big man was too strong and shoved him to the ground. When the limo rounded the bend in the alley,

Bull was locked in indecision between shooting Johnny or the limo, but when the vehicle kept coming, he turned to fire at it.

Brakes squealed as the gun went off, but the bullet went high as the limo slammed into Bull and sent him flying backwards, to land on his butt near the dumpster.

Johnny snatched up the fallen gun and walked over to stand above Bull, who was cradling his broken right leg. Bull gazed up at him, and then raised a hand in pleading.

"No, don't!"

Johnny fired two shots, one that struck Bull in the head, while the other hit his heart.

When he had dealt with the traitor, he turned to see Merle and Earl gawking at him.

"You boys just saved my life, consider your pay doubled, and shut and lock the gates."

Merle and Earl were still staring at Bull's body when Johnny went back inside to make calls.

"Merle."

"Yeah?"

"Don't tell Johnny that your foot just slipped off the pedal, okay?"

"Okay."

***

Despite the early morning hour, the doorbell rang at Laurel Ivy's townhouse.

Pullo was staying over, and he went with Laurel to see who had come to call and woken them up.

It was Laurel's nurse, Maya, a young Asian woman, and her eyes looked red from crying.

"Maya, what's wrong?"

"I'm so sorry, Laurel, but I really need to speak to you, and it can't wait until morning."

Pullo yawned as he walked off towards the kitchen.

"I'll let you two talk while I get a drink of water."

After Pullo walked down the short hallway and disappeared into the kitchen, Maya reached into her jacket pocket and took out a gun.

Laurel backed away from her so fast that she bumped the entryway table and knocked over a vase.

"Maya... why?"

"A man offered me money, so much money, to kill Joe, but... I can't leave a witness, I'm sorry."

An instant later, Maya had dropped the gun and was gagging on the carving knife that Pullo had thrown from the kitchen doorway.

Eight inches of razor sharp stainless steel entered her throat, severed her trachea, and cut off her air supply.

For several moments, Laurel simply watched in shock and horror, but as Maya began thrashing about on the floor, and desperately ripped the knife from her throat in an attempt to get air, Laurel moved towards her to help, but was held back by Pullo, who grabbed up the gun and kicked the knife from Maya's hand.

"Let the bitch die," Pullo said.

Laurel did so, but refrained from watching it take place, as she buried her face against Pullo's chest and cried.

It took several minutes, but Maya died, and as if to mark her passing, Pullo's cell phone began ringing upstairs in the bedroom.

He placed an arm around Laurel's shoulders and led her up the steps, and then grabbed the phone off the nightstand and answered it on the sixteenth ring.

It was Johnny, who had just survived his own attack and betrayal.

Pullo told him what had just happened, and they agreed to meet at the club.

Minutes later, Pullo and Laurel were in his Hummer and headed away from her townhouse.

Laurel had stopped shaking, and took out her phone.

"Should I call Tanner? Is this what he was talking about when he gave me his number?"

"I don't think he expected this, not an attack by a friend, but yeah, I guess he didn't put anything past Heinz."

"They wanted you dead, not me. Maya was just going to kill me because I was a witness, and, what do we do with her body?"

"I'll have it taken care of, and the next time you go home, there won't be a sign of trouble."

"Oh my God, I nearly died. You saved me, Joe."

"I heard the vase break, if not for that…"

"Should I call, Tanner?"

"Yeah, tell him what happened and have him meet us at the club."

***

Tanner had assigned Laurel's number a special ring, and he awoke from a sound sleep after it rang only once.

"Laurel, are you alright?"

She wasn't, and he could hear the tears in her voice as she told him what had happened. Afterwards, she passed the phone and Pullo filled him in on the attempt on Johnny's life as well, and told him that they would all meet at the club, where they would plan a counter attack.

After ending the call, Tanner saw that Sophia had awakened and was staring at him.

"That was that doctor?"

"Heinz sent someone to her home to kill Pullo... and her."

"Shit, are they alright?"

"Yeah, Joe handled it, also, someone tried to kill Rossetti, one of his own people, but he's okay too, but they were all very lucky."

Tanner grew silent as Sophia put on a light and rose from the bed.

"We're safe here, right?"

"Yes, but we're leaving anyway. Rossetti wants to meet at the club."

Sophia put on her robe and went into the bathroom, and when she emerged a minute later, she saw that Tanner hadn't moved, but that his face had grown red with rage.

"Tanner... are you alright?"

He stood and grabbed his clothes.

"Get dressed, I'm putting you in a cab and sending you to the club."

"Where are you going?"

Tanner's intense eyes blazed, and Sophia spotted the hate burning in them.

"I'm going back to that hotel of Heinz's, and I'm going to kill them all."

***

Sophia pleaded with Tanner not to face Heinz's men alone, but her appeals to reason fell on deaf ears, and after seeing that she was in a taxi and on her way to the club, Tanner drove six blocks and entered an underground parking garage.

The attendant was in the middle of telling him that he couldn't park his car himself, when Tanner told him to pull up a file on the company computer. The young man gave him a strange look, but when the file was found, the man saw that it contained a photo of Tanner, and that it identified him as one of the owners of the property.

He wasn't the owner, but had made a deal with the woman who did own it, and the deal allowed him a permanent parking space in several of the garages she owned. In the space at this garage was a van, and that van held supplies and an arsenal.

In ten minutes, Tanner had donned body armor and wore a tactical vest over it.

He parked in the alley that ran behind the Rutherford Hotel and left the car carrying an AR-15, while an Atchisson assault shotgun was slung across his back. The tactical vest held a Beretta in its holster, and there were spare magazines and shells for the three weapons.

He entered the hotel by the same second-story window he'd left it by the day before, after kicking in the plywood that had been fastened in place over it.

The noise brought three men stumbling into the hall with eyes puffy from sleep, and Tanner shot them all and went looking for more. Only one man had been wise enough to carry a gun, but he never got off a shot

Tanner assumed that Heinz would be in his suite, on the top floor of the sixth story building, but needed to clear it before heading up, and so he went downstairs to the ground floor, and was met by a group of men who had been playing a late-night game of poker.

Tanner opened up with the AR-15 on full automatic and killed three of the six men right away. As he reloaded, two bullets struck him in the chest, and despite the body armor, the pain was maddening, and caused his eyes to tear up.

Tanner blinked the water of pain away and opened fire again, this time using three-round bursts, and after killing another man, the last two dived behind the oak reception counter.

If they had hoped that the massive and ornate service desk would protect them, they were sorely mistaken, and the ammo from the AR-15, the .223 Remingtons ripped through the wood, the men, and the wall behind them.

After clearing the ground floor, Tanner heard the sound of footsteps on the stairs, but to his amazement, the elevator chimed, and the old man who had been wearing the bathrobe the previous night emerged from the machine wearing the same again, but this time he was carrying a shotgun.

Tanner hit him with a burst from the AR-15, and the fool fell back into the elevator car with his feet sticking out and the shotgun laying atop his body, while the doors of the elevator repeatedly opened and closed upon his legs.

Tanner took off at a run up the stairs, and began firing the instant he spotted movement.

There were four men in their underwear on the second-floor landing and his shots caught them in their bare legs, taking the fight out of all but one of them, and that man fired a shot that hit the web of flesh between the thumb and forefinger on Tanner's left hand, causing it to drip blood and sting like a sonofabitch.

Tanner shot the man in the face and moved on, as the other three men moaned in agony from their wounds. Two of the men he recognized as his drinking companions from the night before, but he felt no pity for them, not after Laurel Ivy had nearly been killed.

As he opened the door to the third floor, the floor where most of the men were housed, Tanner got what he expected, as a brutal barrage of gunfire perforated the metal door with over a dozen holes, while four more rounds found Tanner's vest, knocking the breath from his lungs.

Tanner recovered quickly, and his intent had not been to enter the floor, but to deliver a surprise and shut the door again.

The grenade exploded and the door blew open and hung from one hinge, as the bottom hinge had been blown off by the explosion, even as the blast ripped apart several men.

Tanner slid the rifle around the edge of the doorframe and emptied its final magazine down the corridor, before trading the AR-15 for the Atchisson assault shotgun. Particles of debris and dust filled the air, but Tanner could make out four torn bodies lying atop the carpet, with two more casualties farther down the corridor.

That meant that he had encountered twenty men since entering the building, and he knew from his stay at the hotel the day before that there should be at least two more somewhere, not counting Heinz and Vance.

If the men were hiding, then so be it. Time was short, and doubtless, someone passing nearby the building had heard the noise, and he still had to get to the top floor and kill Heinz before the authorities appeared.

One of the missing men fired at him as he opened the door to the sixth floor, and before he could fire back, the man tackled him, and the two of them went tumbling down the stairs together.

Both the man and Tanner had lost their weapons during the fall down to the landing, and Tanner had also banged his head on the wall as he landed, and was momentarily stunned.

The other man recovered first, and that's when Tanner realized that it was the Frenchman who spoke only a little German.

The Frenchman's eyes also widened in recognition, and he grabbed the weapon nearest to him, pointed it at Tanner, and pulled the trigger.

Nothing happened, because the man had grabbed the AR-15, which was out of ammo.

After realizing his mistake, he made a leap to retrieve his own weapon, which was laying behind him on a stair, but when he turned back around to fire, Tanner tossed a knife that entered his left eye.

The Frenchman screamed in agony, but his pain was short lived, as Tanner ripped the gun from the man's hand and shot him in the head twice.

"Heinz!" Tanner called, and his voice was filled with fury, as he ached to kill the man who had dared to threaten Laurel Ivy's life, but vengeance was to be denied, because when he made it back up the stairs and onto the sixth floor, he found that the suites and conference room were empty.

Heinz had been wise enough to move somewhere else after Tanner's destruction of his hit team, and the assassin would have to wait to get revenge.

Tanner made his way back down the stairs, and found that two of the men wounded on the second floor landing still lived, but were too weak from their wounds to fight, and he shot them with the Beretta to finish them off.

To his surprise, no sirens greeted his ears upon reaching the lobby, but he remembered that the once elegant hotel was well-built, and also surrounded by warehouses which were closed for the night, and that the street saw little traffic after daylight hours.

The sound of the grenade going off might have reached the restaurant on the corner, but he recalled that there was music playing inside, and it was an even chance that no one heard the sound, or if heard, they didn't consider it menacing.

Whatever the reason for the lack of a police response, so much the better, and Heinz could return to find his nest in ruins.

The sound of running footsteps came from the area of the front doors after they crashed open, and Tanner nearly shot Johnny Rossetti and Joe Pullo as they came towards him with their guns up and ready

They both stopped and stared at him, noting the blood dripping from his hand and splattered over his armor and clothing, and their guns fell to their sides.

"Heinz?" Johnny said.

"He's not here, just his men,"

Pullo was swiveling his head about, searching for danger.

"How many men?"

"There should have been at least twenty-two, but I only encountered twenty-one."

Pullo and Johnny glanced at each other, before looking back at Tanner.

"They're all dead?" Johnny asked, and his tone was laced with amazement.

"Yeah," Tanner said.

Johnny nodded at the body of the old man, which was lying in the doorway of the open elevator.

"The old man was unarmed?"

Tanner turned his head to look at the old man's body and saw another man step from the recesses of the elevator holding a shotgun.

Pullo knocked Tanner to the floor, as Johnny raised his weapon and fired.

The twenty-second man had been in the elevator, and had been pointing the old man's shotgun at Tanner's back.

Pullo tackled Tanner, just before the man fired, and the pellets whizzed by overhead, missing the back of Tanner's skull by mere inches, as Johnny fired three rounds into the man and killed him.

Tanner rolled out from beneath Pullo, and the two men sprang up to their feet.

"I guess that was number twenty-two," Johnny said.

"Thanks Rossetti, you too Joe, but what about Sophia, she made it to the club, didn't she?"

"Yeah," Pullo said. "She's why we're here; she said that you were going after Heinz alone, which was stupid, Tanner, even for you."

Tanner looked back at the man Johnny had shot, the one who had nearly blown his head off.

"I can't argue the point, but Heinz needed to know that some things aren't acceptable."

"You're talking about Laurel," Pullo said, and Tanner acknowledged it with a nod.

Johnny turned and headed for the door.

"Let's get out of here."

The three men made their exit and headed back towards the club, leaving behind a slaughterhouse, and a lesson well taught.

CHAPTER 31 - Envious eyes

Tanner had thought he might find Sara Blake at the club, but Johnny explained that he didn't want her to know about the latest attack on his life, as she was still upset that he had nearly been killed once that week.

Tanner was glad she wasn't there, as he had little patience for her, and with the truce in place, he hoped to never see her again.

Johnny had left half a dozen men to guard the club, but Merle and Earl still stood on either side of Laurel like personal sentries, but she came over to Tanner when she spotted the wound to his hand.

Sophia greeted him with a kiss, but when she went to hug him, she felt him tense up, as a hissing sound escaped his lips.

When she rolled up his shirt, she spotted a slew of purple bruises.

"Damn Tanner, how many times were you shot?"

"It's why I wore the body armor,"

Laurel came over with her medical bag and winced at the bruises.

"Oh my God, it looks like you're lucky to be alive; you've also torn your stitches open, and let me see that hand."

"Are you alright, Laurel?"

"I'm a little shaken, but I'll be fine."

"Good,"

Laurel repaired his old stitches and placed new ones in his hand, while also making a face of concern at the bump on the back of his head, which was acquired from his tumble down the stairs with the Frenchman. When she offered him an ointment to put on the bruises, Tanner declined.

Sophia stood off to the side watching them, and Tanner could tell that she was unhappy about Laurel touching him, even if it was in a utilitarian manner.

When he replaced his bloody shirt with a sweatshirt given to him by Johnny, which advertised the club, Sophia stood beside him and thanked Laurel for treating him. Laurel took the hint, and moved away.

Tanner was seated on a stool at the bar, and Sophia moved between his legs and spoke in a quiet voice.

"That bitch wants you."

"Laurel had her fill of me years ago."

"Why?"

"She wanted to be loved, and I couldn't give that to her."

"Commitment scares you, don't I know it, but no one can help falling in love."

Tanner said nothing, but he sincerely hoped that Sophia was wrong.

***

One of Heinz's men had managed to call him before falling to Tanner's onslaught, and he arrived at the hotel with Vance just minutes after Tanner had left the building with Johnny and Pullo.

Heinz reacted to the scenes of death with amazed and horrified expressions, but Vance's eyes were filled with pure wonder.

"This was Tanner, all of it. I can feel it."

They had been upstairs and were now back down in the lobby, where Heinz turned in a circle while gesturing at the carnage.

"One man, all this?"

"Most of it, I'd bet on it. You can read his trail by the cartridges left behind."

Heinz walked over to a chair and sat in it heavily.

"This is disastrous. My men are all dead."

"You still have the offer from the Russians."

Heinz sighed, the last thing he wanted was a partner, but controlling half of something was better than not having control over any of it.

"I'll meet with the Russian, this Michael Krupin, but I want to maintain control as well."

"I'll tell him you're ready to talk, but he'll want to know what you can add to the deal. Are you certain you know the inner workings of the Giacconi Family's enterprises?"

"I do, and with that information, and the Russian's men, we'll make an unbeatable pair."

Vance nodded. Knowledge was power, and he began to wonder just how much it would take to extract that knowledge from Heinz's bald head.

He had been Richards' lackey, and had now become Heinz's; perhaps it was time that he started working for himself.

His musing about upper mobility was interrupted by Heinz speaking again.

"I have to stay alive long enough to meet with the Russian, and that means that I have to avoid Tanner."

"I'll buy time. I'll meet with Rossetti and pretend you want to compromise."

"The man will kill you. They must know that I'm without men now, and to that point, how do I dispose of these bodies before they're discovered by the authorities?"

"Such services can be bought, although, they're not cheap, particularly when dealing in a quantity such as this."

Heinz held his head in his hands.

"This war will bankrupt me if this keeps up."

"No, and as soon as you make the deal with Krupin, we'll attack Rossetti's businesses. By tomorrow night, you'll own every brothel, drug den, and bookmaking operation now run by the Giacconi's, and once Rossetti has fallen, the others will get back in line and The Conglomerate will be in control once again.

Heinz seemed invigorated by Vance's words, but doubt still clouded his expression.

"What if Rossetti kills you at the meeting?"

"He won't. He thinks he has nothing to lose by talking to me."

"Set up the meeting with Rossetti, and if you never return from it… I'll assume that things went badly."

Vance laughed.

"Yes, that would be a safe assumption."

***

The intercom buzzed in the office at the club, and Johnny was informed that he had a call. When he answered it, he heard a voice he remembered well.

It was Vance, whose real name was Rurik Varanov.

"Why the call, comrade? I hope you're not looking for work; I don't hire assholes."

"It's good to hear your voice again as well, Rossetti, but I'm calling to set up a meeting, Bruno Heinz has empowered me to seek peace with you."

"Peace talks? I'm not surprised, Tanner put more than a little dent in Heinz's forces."

"On the contrary, it's I who have put a dent in Tanner, or don't you know that he was wounded when we met."

"It's a scratch, and Tanner will pay you back for it someday soon."

"Not if we make peace, so why not meet and talk things over?"

"When and where?"

"I'll show good faith and come to your club at two, and make sure that Tanner is there. It's time that we were properly introduced."

"You're really willing to come here, unarmed?"

"I am, if I have your word that I'll be allowed to leave in one piece."

"You got it, but Vance, if this is a trick, you'll be the first to die."

"No tricks," Vance assured him, and then the line went dead.

Johnny looked over at Tanner, who was sitting on the green sofa with Sophia. The call had been on speakerphone, and he had heard every word of it, along with Pullo, who was seated in front of the desk.

"Will you be at the meeting?"

Tanner stood, and Sophia did likewise.

"I'll be here, and if we're meeting here, I guess that means that you're closing the club. That's a good idea with what has been happening."

Johnny nodded.

"Heinz already sent hitters here once, and I won't put the people that work here or the customers in danger."

Pullo spoke up from where he sat in front of the desk.

"This meeting is a trick. Heinz is just trying to buy time until he can hire more men."

"I know that," Tanner said. "But he's run out of time,"

"You have a plan, don't you?" Johnny said.

"I do, and if it works, Heinz will be too busy fighting the law to worry about anything else."

"Explain that," Johnny said.

Tanner hesitated for a moment. He wasn't used to working as part of a team and sharing his plans, but Rossetti was the man who hired him to put an end to the war with Heinz, and so he didn't see the harm in letting him in on his plans.

"The financial records that Tim Jackson took from Richards' computer also included info on Heinz's money laundering. I'm going to contact that IRS agent that's been sniffing around and hand Heinz over to her."

Johnny looked worried.

"Won't those records implicate us as well?"

"No, Tim Jackson is going to supply me with redacted copies; anything concerning the Giacconi Family will be erased. Also, the IRS will have to pass this on to the German authorities, so he'll have two governments giving him grief."

Johnny grinned.

"That's clever, Tanner, but I want to see this info before you pass it on."

"I'll send it to you as soon as I get it, and after you've seen it, I'll make contact with Agent Taylor."

"If this works, the war will be over by the time we meet Vance for the meeting, good, I want to see his face when he finds out his new employer no longer needs his services."

Laurel appeared in the doorway and spoke to Pullo.

"Is it safe to go home yet?"

Johnny nodded.

"It is, thanks to Tanner, but there will be someone on guard every minute anyway."

Pullo took Laurel by the hand as they left to go to her townhouse, and possibly her bed, and although Tanner tried to hide it, there was a look of envy in his eyes.

CHAPTER 32 - Achilles' heel

Sara slept fitfully that night, and after waking from yet another bad dream, she grabbed her phone and checked the tracker again.

She knew that Tanner was staying at a Midtown hotel with Sophia Verona, but her eyes widened with alarm when she saw that Tanner had been back to the Rutherford Hotel, and in the early morning hours at that.

The alarm escalated to fear, when the tracking data told her that after leaving Heinz, Tanner had traveled to the Cabaret Strip Club, but only stayed there a short time before leaving.

She knew that the club should be closed at the hour of his visit, and in her imagination, she saw Tanner planting a bomb in Rossetti's office.

She cleared her phone's screen and dialed Johnny's phone.

"Sara, why are you awake so early?"

"Are you alright? Has something happened?"

There was a pause, and after sighing, Johnny answered.

"There was some trouble, but we handled it, and how did you find out?"

"Where are you?"

"I'm still at the club, but getting ready to leave."

"What sort of trouble? Did someone try to kill you again?"

"Yes, and Joe too, but don't worry, we're all safe."

"It was Tanner."

Johnny laughed.

"It wasn't Tanner, trust me on that, and I thought you weren't going to think about him anymore."

"Tanner and Heinz are working together behind your back. That's why you and Joe were attacked when he was nowhere around. He wanted to claim his innocence, and once you were dead, he would kill me."

"Sara, calm down. You're way off base, Tanner is on our side."

Sara wanted to tell him about tracking Tanner's movements, but knew that it would just make him angry, and that he'd accuse her of breaking her word to leave Tanner alone. He would be right of course, but it was obvious to her that Tanner had no intention of keeping his word, and so she felt justified. Still, it was best if she didn't share that knowledge yet, or else Johnny might tell Tanner about the tracker.

"Don't trust him, Johnny, and if it's proof you need, I'll get it."

"Listen, I'm dead tired and have to sleep, but I'll come by your place later tonight and we'll talk."

"Don't go to your apartment. Stay at a hotel instead."

"I'm just going to catch a few hours of sleep on the sofa in my office, and calm down. You don't have to fear Tanner anymore."

"Don't trust him. Promise me that you won't be alone with him."

"I promise, now go back to sleep, it's early, and hey?"

"Yes?"

"I love you, baby."

Sara grinned at hearing those words, and for a moment, Tanner was forgotten.

"I love you too, Johnny."

After they said goodbye, Sara knew that she'd never go back to sleep. She activated the tracker software again, and saw that Tanner had returned to his hotel.

Sara headed for the shower. She would keep a watchful eye on Tanner, and the next time he met with Heinz, she would get close and take pictures, that way, Johnny would have to believe her, and it would justify her spying on the man as well.

In less than an hour, she was dressed, had eaten a light breakfast, and was parked three blocks from Tanner's hotel. She didn't need to tail him closely, because the tracker would do the work for her.

She knew that if she called the police or FBI that Tanner would be arrested, but had little faith that the man could be held captive for long.

He had escaped a Mexican prison and a locked jail cell in the time she'd been after him, and if the legal system was ever foolish enough to grant bail to the man, he would surely flee, only to return when least expected, and kill her.

No, Tanner was too dangerous to be left alive, and taking his word for anything was insane as far as Sara was concerned.

Nothing had changed.

Tanner had to die.

And once she had proof that the man's word was worthless, she would be free to use any means at her disposal to bring about his death.

And, in fact, she had already put such a plan in motion.

CHAPTER 33 - Plan to be lucky

On the Upper East Side of Manhattan, Vance met with Michael Krupin inside Krupin's limo.

Michael Krupin was twenty-three, with dark good looks, but rarely smiled. He wore a suit worth more than most wardrobes, and there was an air of entitlement about him.

Vance had been friends with his father and had known Michael since he was a boy. The boy was a man now, and the man craved power.

"Heinz, the German, can he be trusted?" Krupin asked.

"He can be trusted," Vance said. "But I'll be your partner, not Heinz,"

Krupin stared at Vance as he pondered the meaning behind those words. Michael Krupin was a young man, but he had an older man's patience and rarely spoke without thinking things through beforehand.

"You have plans for Heinz?"

"I do."

"And if those plans work out, I suppose the German will never see his homeland again."

"Thanks to Tanner, Heinz has no more people around to protect him, but the man does have something of value."

"And what would that be?" Krupin asked.

"He has knowledge, and once I get it out of him, I'll have knowledge."

"And so you want a partnership, is that it?"

"Yes, I want a percentage of everything now controlled by the Giacconi Family."

"That's quite a lot, their marijuana importing is worth over a hundred million a year, but that's because they have a strong distribution network. If possible, I would like to keep Rossetti's people in place, at least in the beginning, and later on, we'll move our people in."

"Our people? So you're saying we have a deal?"

"By 'our people', I meant the Russian people, but yes, if you give me a blueprint of the Giacconi Family's inner workings, their systems, and what properties they own, if you deliver all that, we have a deal."

"I'll get it, and I'll also kill Tanner."

Michael Krupin almost smiled at Vance.

"Please deliver the information to me before you go against Tanner, otherwise, you just might take it to your grave."

"You should have more confidence in me, Michael. Tanner is great, but I'm better, and once I kill him, everyone will know it."

"You could try to recruit him. I'd be willing to pay serious money to have a man with his skills, if even half of what I've heard is true."

"It's true. You should see what he did to Heinz's men last night."

"Could you have done the same?"

Vance laughed.

"Face twenty men on my own? I wouldn't be stupid enough to try."

"So you think he's a lucky fool?"

"I certainly hope so, and I also hope that luck comes to an end if I ever have to face him."

"I prefer planning over luck," Krupin said.

"So do I, but if I had to choose, I'd choose luck."

"But we don't get to choose, do we?"

Vance thought about Frank Richards, and how close the man had come to gaining undreamed of power and influence, only to have his ambitions, and his life, snuffed out by Tanner.

"No, sometimes fate just isn't on our side."

CHAPTER 34 - Wheels within wheels

Tanner persuaded Jade Taylor to meet with him by telling her he had information about money laundering, and they arranged to rendezvous at an outdoor cafe near Central Park, which also offered a view of the famous Dakota Building.

He had told her on the phone that his name was Smith, and Jade Taylor said that many men named Smith had passed on information to her over the years.

Pullo had described Jade Taylor to Tanner, and so he spotted her right away and joined her at a table. After saying hello, they both ordered coffee from a waitress already wielding a carafe, and once it was poured, they ignored it and got down to business.

Tanner was actually pressed for time, as it took longer than planned for the information to be formatted without referencing anyone but Heinz, and then Johnny had to peruse it before giving approval.

The time for meeting with Vance at the club was coming up fast, and Tanner planned to be there.

Jade Taylor offered Tanner a guarded smile.

"Mr. Smith, exactly what is it that you wish to pass on to me?"

Tanner slid a flash drive across the table with a gloved hand.

"Have you heard of The Conglomerate?" Tanner said.

"I've heard rumors," Jade said.

"The rumors are true, and there's information on that drive detailing the laundering of money by one of its members, although, The Conglomerate is actually in shambles now."

Jade studied the drive in her hand.

"What do you want in return?"

"Other than swift action, not a thing, but perhaps I'll get a warm feeling from being a good citizen." Tanner stood and pointed at the untouched beverages. "I'll let Uncle Sam pay for the coffee."

Seconds later, and Tanner had disappeared into the crowd.

Jade Taylor rose from her seat, dropped money on the table, and walked off in the opposite direction. After turning a corner, she walked two blocks, and stepped inside a van that was waiting for her.

Once the van pulled into traffic, Jade removed the wireless transmitter hidden beneath her hair and asked the driver if the conversation had recorded.

"We got it all, and the client will be very pleased with your performance. Tanner is not an easy man to fool, and neither are Pullo and Rossetti."

"I was so tempted to just shoot him. I can't believe that he gave you so much trouble the other night."

"Don't underestimate the man; everyone who has is dead, and you can't spend the bounty if you're dead."

"What bounty?"

"There was fifty grand up for whoever killed him, and no one even came close."

"The client, whoever they are, they're still willing to pay to see him dead, right?"

"Oh yeah, now that Tanner has proven he can't be trusted all bets are off, but don't get any ideas, the man would eat you alive."

The van stopped in front of Grand Central Terminal.

"You did good work playing Jade Taylor, June, now take the train back to Connecticut and I'll contact you soon, and oh yeah, expect a bonus."

Special Agent Jade Taylor, who was actually a con woman named June Thompson, stepped out of the van and walked towards the terminal's entrance.

The driver of the van moved back into traffic and activated his Bluetooth to make a call.

Sara Blake answered on the first ring.

"Duke?"

"You were right! Tanner is trying to sell out Rossetti to the Feds, and I've not only got the conversation on tape, but also the evidence he passed along to our phony IRS agent."

There was an audible sigh of relief and then Sara spoke again.

"I knew that bastard wouldn't keep his word, and now it's time to put an end to him."

"What's your plan?"

"I'm not sure, any suggestions?"

"Yes, let Rossetti handle Tanner. Tanner won't expect anything to come of the information he passed on until later today, and there's a window of opportunity where he'll think Rossetti still knows nothing."

"No. That's too risky, unless… Tanner trusts Joe Pullo, and maybe Pullo can kill him. He'd be wise to anyway. I think Tanner wants that doctor he's seeing."

"Fine, pass on what you know to Rossetti and have him give the job to Pullo, with any luck, Tanner will never see it coming."

CHAPTER 35 - All ears

Tanner arrived back at the club just moments before Robert Vance appeared.

Before his arrival, Johnny had received an email on his phone that contained the audio recording of Tanner's conversation with the phony IRS agent, Jade Taylor, but he didn't have time to listen to it before the meeting.

Sara had written a short note to go with it.

Call me back after you listen to this and I'll explain.

Love, Sara

Although curious, Johnny had to hold off listening to the recording, because of Vance's arrival.

Pullo patted Vance down for weapons, and found that he had none.

Johnny was standing with his back against the bar, and Vance sent him a nod, but then he stared at Tanner, who was seated at one of the tables.

"Why didn't Heinz come himself?" Johnny asked.

"I am the one you will deal with, Rossetti, and what's that saying, I have his ear?"

Vance walked over and stood before Tanner.

"Hello Tanner, although we traded shots in the hallway at MegaZenith, and again at the Rutherford Hotel, I can't say that we were formally introduced, also, I believe you were masquerading as someone else at MegaZenith."

"You should talk, Vance?" Johnny said. "Or should we call you, Rurik Varanov?"

Vance smiled, and turned towards Johnny.

"As a matter of fact, Rossetti, I've recently embraced my Russian roots, and I've made contact with an old friend. Perhaps you know him, Mikhail Krupin?"

"The leader of the Russian mob, what about him?"

"He has agreed to lend a hand in Heinz's crusade to take over the city, as a partner of course,"

"Krupin has thrown in with Heinz? If that's true, he's just made a big mistake, and so have you. Heinz is soon to be history."

"Actually, Heinz is already history. The old fool was powerless without his men."

"You've pushed Heinz out?" Pullo said.

Vance slowly reached into an inside pocket, and when his hand emerged, he was holding a handkerchief, which, when he opened it, contained a severed human ear.

Vance grinned.

"When I said I had Heinz's ear, I meant it. You're now dealing with me, Rossetti, and I've got Mikhail Krupin backing me up."

Johnny made a face as he took in the blood-speckled ear, but then shook his head in disagreement.

"Krupin is too smart to start trouble, not after all the losses we both had in the last war."

Vance tucked the ear back in his pocket as he spoke.

"That's ancient history, and I'm talking about the son, Mikhail Krupin Jr., who goes by the name Michael, not the father, who, unfortunately, suffered a serious stroke recently. Unfortunate for you that is, very fortunate for me, as the son is more adventurous."

Johnny smiled as he tried to appear unconcerned.

"If the kid wants a war, he'll have one, and his men will wind up the same as Heinz's men."

Vance spoke to Tanner again.

"Speaking of that, that massacre at the Rutherford, that was all you, wasn't it?"

"All but one," Tanner said.

Vance grinned with pleasure.

"Magnificent, and someday, it will be just you and me,"

"Anytime you're ready," Tanner said.

"I'm always ready, Tanner, but I don't want to overstay my welcome, or tempt anyone to forget their pledge to keep things civilized."

Vance headed for the door.

"You'll be hearing from us."

After Vance left, Johnny thumped the top of the bar with his fist.

"Damn it! Just when we had Heinz where we wanted him, Vance has to change the players."

"What's this mean? More trouble, or less?" Tanner asked.

"More," Joe said. "The Russians outnumber us bigtime. It's out of the frying pan and into the fire."

Johnny walked over and looked down at Tanner.

"Are you still with us?"

"Yes, Rossetti, same deal,"

"Call me Johnny, Tanner, after all, we've saved each other's lives, although, I still owe you one."

Tanner stood and offered his hand.

"Johnny it is,"

They shook, and Johnny moved behind the bar. After opening three bottles of beer, Johnny slid two of them towards Pullo, who handed one to Tanner, where he had retaken his seat at the table.

Johnny held up his bottle.

"The Russians are coming, let's make them wish they were never born."

CHAPTER 36 - How hard can it be?

June Thompson, the con woman who had pretended to be Special Agent Jade Taylor, left the train station and hailed a taxi.

Fifty grand, fifty thousand dollars for killing just one man,

June had killed men before, the first time to survive, as the man who taught her how to be a grifter was prone to violence when he was drunk.

That proclivity to harm women began to show itself when he wasn't drinking, and the man tried to rape her, after he'd grown angry at her latest refusal to sleep with him.

June killed the fool with a knife she kept in her purse, and then ran to her lover for help. Her lover at the time was an older female grifter named Annie, and Annie helped young June dispose of the body.

Later in life, one of her marks caught on that he was being swindled, and June killed him before he could call the police.

That time she had used a gun, a weapon she later planted inside the car belonging to the man's estranged wife. As far as June knew, the wife was still serving a life sentence.

There had been two other men as well, partners in a complicated con, and she and the other woman involved in the scheme killed the men.

They had overheard the men planning to cheat them out of their share of their ill-gotten gains, and so they shot them together as the men were watching a ballgame, and then of course, June turned the gun on the other woman and killed her as well.

The woman had a tendency to run her mouth, and June didn't want to take a chance. At least, that's what she told herself, and it left her alone with all the money.

June had studied Tanner when they met, and she found him to be unimpressive. While he was of a good height, six foot or so, he was hardly a big man, and she marveled that so many people had failed at killing him.

When they were sitting at the table, she was tempted to just take out her gun and shoot him. It would have been so easy.

After Duke dropped her off at the terminal, she bought her ticket, fully intending to use it, but she couldn't get Tanner out of her mind.

Fifty thousand dollars, just to kill Tanner, amazing,

When her train was called, June sat unmoving, and it left the station without her.

She had been thinking, thinking of how easy it would be to just walk up to Tanner while he still believed that she was the law, and blast his ass into next week.

Two minutes after her train left the station, she had a plan in mind, a simple plan.

Find Tanner and shoot him dead.

For after all, how hard could it be?

CHAPTER 37 - Unintended consequences

Johnny, Pullo, and Tanner, were on their second beers, and the talk had veered away from business and onto sports.

Tanner knew that Joe Pullo was a football fan, but Johnny Rossetti surprised him by having a vast knowledge of the sport.

"Oh yeah, Tanner, I almost never miss the Giants when they play at home, and I was also a quarterback in high school. I wasn't very good though, and we lost most of our games, but man I loved playing."

Pullo then spoke of the day he first met Tanner, when the hit man delivered the severed head of mob informant, Vincenzo Righettleto, to the funeral parlor owned by Sam Giacconi.

Tanner looked around at the club.

"This is that same building, isn't it?"

Johnny nodded.

"It is. Sam sold it to me cheap when he got out of the funeral home business, and when I told him that I was opening a strip club, he said that the place was going from dealing with bones, to dealing with boners."

"The place had been a bar anyway before it was a funeral parlor," Pullo said. "And back in the 1920s it was a speakeasy."

"The place has some history attached," Tanner agreed.

Johnny's phone rang while he was leaning on the bar and talking about the Pop Warner Football team he helped to sponsor. Both Tanner and Pullo were seated at a table just a few feet away.

It was Sara calling from her apartment, and Johnny excused himself and moved down along the bar.

"Did you get my message?"

"I did, but I haven't had a chance to listen to it. What is it?"

"It's proof that Tanner isn't keeping his word. He met with the woman he believed was an IRS agent, and tried to pass on evidence that you've been money laundering."

Johnny moved even farther down the bar, where he couldn't be overheard.

"What do you mean that Tanner *believed* she was an IRS agent, are you saying she's not?"

"I... I hired her, through Duke. Once I learned that Tanner had information that he could use to hurt you, I placed her there to make it easy for him to do so, and today I was proven right."

Johnny moaned.

"What was that groan about?" Sara said.

"Tanner went to Jade Taylor for me; we were going to use her to take down Heinz. Didn't you even look at what he gave her?"

"I... hold on, let me load this in my laptop."

As he waited for Sara to view the file, Johnny looked over at Tanner, who was talking to Pullo. Sara had crossed the line again, but with luck, Tanner would never find out about it.

When Sara came back on the phone, she sounded confused.

"You're right; this file is all about Heinz and his company's activities here and in Germany."

"Yes, Sara, now please, let it go. Tanner isn't trying to outsmart or double-cross us. He just wants you to leave him alone, and so do I."

"No, no, there's more than this, much more. Tanner is working with Heinz, he must be, the man spent the night at that hotel where Heinz lives."

"Yes, he did, he infiltrated Heinz's headquarters and killed an elite team of assassins the next day, and last night he went back and finished the rest of Heinz's men off."

"Are you certain?"

"I was there last night. Sara, he killed over twenty men by himself. Joe thinks that he became enraged because Laurel was nearly killed when Heinz tried to kill Joe."

"You think that Tanner really cares for her?"

"I don't think anything is going on, nothing like that, but from what I hear, they have a past, but, wait a second, how did you know that Tanner spent the night in that hotel?"

There was no answer, although Johnny could hear her breathing.

"Sara?"

"The other night, Duke, he managed to place a tracker on Tanner, and, I've been following his movements."

"Jesus,"

"I know, but I don't trust him."

"You gave your word that you were through hounding the man. Doesn't that mean anything, Sara?"

"Of course it does, but I wasn't going to blindly trust that his word was just as good."

"Honey, from where I'm sitting, it's better."

There was silence, and then, Sara spoke in a resigned tone.

"I'll tell Duke to stand down, and Tanner never has to know about any of this."

The door to the club swung open, and Johnny watched as the woman he knew as Jade Taylor walked in and headed towards Tanner with a smile on her face.

"Your phony IRS agent is back, what's that about?"

"She's there?"

"Yeah, you didn't send her?"

"No, Duke said that she was on a train."

"Shit, she's got a gun!"

Sara heard a string of gunfire, such as the sound a fully automatic weapon made while firing, and then the clatter of the phone as it hit the floor.

Afterwards, she could hear someone shouting, but could only distinguish the voice as male, and that was followed by a woman screaming. The screaming ended, to be replaced by the sound of weeping. More muffled voices, the shouted word of, "Don't!" spoken in a woman's tone, and sounding desperate, and finally, silence.

"Johnny! Johnny what happened? Is Tanner dead? Did she shoot him? Johnny!"

Over a minute passed, and then Sara heard the shuffle of feet. That sound was followed by the sound of crying, but it was the deep soulful cry of a man in mourning.

She shouted into the phone once more, and seconds later, she was rewarded by a voice answering, Tanner's voice.

"Blake?"

"Tanner? What happened? What's going on there?"

"Rossetti is dead... Johnny is dead, murdered by the bitch you sent to kill me."

"No! You're lying! Johnny, put Johnny on the phone."

"Blake!"

"Tell me he's not really dead, please? Oh God, please tell me he's alive."

"I'm coming, Blake."

The phone went dead, and inside her apartment, Sara collapsed to the floor and wept.

CHAPTER 38 - It makes the world go around

Tanner's hands had been resting atop the table when June Thompson, known as IRS agent Jade Taylor, brought up the Glock 19, which had been concealed behind her purse.

The gun held sixteen rounds in total, and had been modified to fire fully automatic.

Tanner had wondered why the IRS agent would be at the club, but hadn't felt threatened by her presence.

June was smiling, half of it was a ruse, while the other half was joy at how easy the hit would be, as she saw no weapon near Tanner's hands, and was glad that she hadn't believed the stories about the man being a killing machine.

By the end of the day, she expected to be fifty-thousand dollars richer; however, she wouldn't live to see the end of the day, or even the next five minutes.

When Tanner saw the gun emerge, he kicked the empty chair that was opposite him, and it slammed into June's legs with enough force to knock her off-balance, even as her finger tightened on the trigger of the gun and sent bullets flying about the bar.

At the same instant that Tanner had kicked the chair at her, Joe Pullo had flung his beer bottle at June, and it struck her in the forehead and shattered, and between that, and the impact of the chair, June fell backwards and became tangled amid the barstools.

Tanner was on her in a flash, to rip the gun from her hand, before landing a solid kick into her stomach.

"Johnny!"

Pullo cried out his friend's name in shock and fear, as he saw that Johnny Rossetti was sprawled on his back near the middle of the bar, and when Pullo reached him, he viewed the line of bloody holes stitched across his friend's torso, and knew that he was dead.

There had been two men guarding the front door, and they were mostly there to shoo away people, while informing them that the bar was closed for the day.

June had made her way past them with the help of her phony Federal Credentials, and one of the men had seen her at the club before and believed she was an agent.

The two men entered the club and stood looking about helplessly at the tragic scene, and Tanner instructed them to go back outside and make sure that no one else entered.

One of the men looked like he wanted to be sick when he realized that Johnny was dead, but he and the other man returned to their post on shaky legs.

June had vomited in reaction to Tanner's kick, and was bent over at the waist, but he gripped her one-handed around the neck and jerked her head up.

"Who do you work for?"

June spat up blood.

"I think you broke something inside me."

"You *think* I broke something? Let's leave no doubts."

Tanner gripped June's right arm with one hand behind her elbow, while the other grabbed her wrist, and then he brought her arm down hard atop his knee. The bones in her forearm made a dry, cracking sound as they splintered, and June let out a scream as her wide eyes took in the bone jutting from her torn and bloody flesh.

For long seconds, the only sound in the bar was that of weeping, the pain-filled whimpering of June, along with the agonizing sobs of grief coming from Pullo.

After June had swallowed several big gulps of air, Tanner questioned her again.

"Who do you work for?"

"I... I was, I was hired by a man named Duke, and he works for someone else, I don't know who."

"I do," Tanner said, as he looked along the bar, where Pullo sat on the floor, cradling Johnny's body in his arms, and he knew that Rossetti's death was caused by Sara.

Tanner grabbed June by the hair, flipped her over onto her stomach, and with one smooth move, he reached around and sliced open her throat with the top half of the jagged beer bottle.

June had spotted the shard of brown glass in Tanner's hand, and cried out for mercy by shouting the word, "Don't!"

There's was no mercy, for however improbable and nascent the friendship between himself and Rossetti had been, it had been forming, and Tanner had grown to like the man.

After slitting her throat, Tanner left June to die in agony, as she gagged and thrashed like a fish without water, while her lifeblood spread into a puddle around her.

Afterwards, Tanner knelt beside Pullo with a hand on his shoulder, and when he heard Sara's tinny voice come from Johnny's phone, he picked it up, and informed her of Johnny's death, while insinuating that she would soon join him in the afterlife.

Pullo took a deep breath, and managed to gasp out words from a face covered in tears.

"Sara did this? She sent that woman to kill you?"

"I don't know if she was sent by Blake, but she worked for her, and as far as I'm concerned, she's broken our truce."

"Oh God, Tanner, look at him, he must have been hit six times." Pullo gazed over at June, who had died, and lay in her own blood. "Oh, you, fucking, bitch!"

Tanner squeezed Pullo's shoulder, stood, and took out his phone.

When Sophia answered, he asked her to take a taxi to the club.

"What's going on?"

"Johnny Rossetti is dead; I'm sorry, Sophia."

"What? How?"

"Sara Blake, someone working for her, but it was an accident. The woman was gunning for me."

Tanner heard Sophia sobbing, and he let her cry until she was able to talk again.

"I loved him, Tanner, you know? I wasn't in love with him anymore, but I still loved him, and he was a hell of a friend."

"I know, but please come, Joe needs someone, and I have to go soon."

"Are you alright?"

"I will be once Blake is dead. This was her doing, and this shit ends today."

"I'll be there as soon as I can," Sophia said, and then the call ended.

Tanner sat on a barstool, looked about the club, then, back down at Rossetti's lifeless form, and realized that the man had been killed because of the actions of the woman he loved, actions spawned from the woman's loss of a previous lover, whose death she sought to avenge.

If it weren't so tragic, the irony would almost be humorous.

CHAPTER 39 - Confession

Thanks to the tracking device hidden on the bottom of Tanner's boot, Sara was able to stay one step ahead of him, and also knew that he had already been to both hers, and Johnny Rossetti's apartment while looking for her.

Oh, Johnny,

Sara was devastated by Rossetti's death, and realized that she was to blame for it. Tanner had been telling the truth when he gave his word that he wouldn't kill her, and had she not sought to trap him in a lie, Johnny would still be living.

At one point in the day, she called the club and spoke to Joe Pullo while crying.

Pullo listened as she told him everything, even revealing that she had planted a tracking device on Tanner. As Johnny had earlier, Pullo realized that she had more knowledge than she should about Tanner's movements over the last few days, and so she admitted the offense.

"Johnny is dead because of you, Sara."

"I know, Joe."

"I think he loved you, and because of that, I won't harm you, but I can't say the same for Tanner, and I won't stand in his way."

"I fucked up, Joe, plain and simple. I gave my word and I broke it, but I just could not imagine that Tanner would keep his word."

"You know, you see Tanner as this great evil, but he's not. He just kills people for a living because it's what he's good at, like a military sniper, and believe it or not, he's about the best man I know."

There was silence on the line after that, but Pullo ended it.

"Goodbye Sara, I don't think I'll be seeing you again."

"Goodbye Joe, and I'm so, so, sorry,"

Just minutes later, the tracker went dead.

Sara had called from the passenger seat of a van driven by Duke, who assumed that he too was on Tanner's kill list.

However, they had a plan, one devised by Sara.

Tanner had to die, but first, Tanner had to be survived.

And as she spent the day hiding from Tanner, a plan had formed on just how to accomplish that, a bold plan, and perhaps a foolish one, because for her plan to work, Tanner would have to be capable of love, and that love, that caring for another human being would prove to be his Achilles' heel.

Is it possible for the Devil to love? Sara asked herself.

If it wasn't, she knew that she might be living her last hours on earth.

CHAPTER 40 - It ends!

Laurel had learned of Johnny's death from Joe, but had been unable to leave the clinic because she had patients that needed treatment, and due to her nurse's treachery, she was working alone.

She had liked Johnny a great deal, as had most of those who knew him, and his death saddened her.

Merle and Earl had been with her earlier in the day, but after Johnny's death, Pullo had asked them to come back to the club, because they would be needed to perform various chores, and also fulfill their duties as chauffeurs.

As darkness fell, Laurel had just finished with her last patient, a leg breaker from the docks who had met up with a late payer who fought back.

The deadbeat had broken three fingers on the collection man's left hand, but the leg breaker had stayed true to his name, and had broken his adversary's kneecaps in retaliation.

Pullo had left a man to guard Laurel, although he didn't believe that she was in any real danger, as she had not been the target of Heinz's would-be assassin, but only a bystander who needed to be dealt with by necessity.

The guard escorted the last patient out, and after watching the gate close behind the departing vehicle, he stayed out front for a smoke.

There was a van parked across from the fence with no one in it, and the guard, named J.T., idly wondered who had left it there, as he puffed away.

But, his mind was occupied by thoughts of the coming days, because with Johnny Rossetti gone and war on the horizon, the Giacconi Family were looking at dark times ahead.

As he was about to go back inside, he spotted the woman walking towards him from the right.

She was beautiful, had long dark hair, and was unbuttoning her blouse as she drew closer.

With his eyes riveted to the ever-increasing exposure of soft flesh, J.T. never noticed Duke coming up on him from the left.

Duke pressed a gun against the J.T.'s head and issued instructions.

"Open the gate with your remote and then punch in the access code for the door, or so help me, I'll blow your head off."

J.T. was a practical sort, and was much wiser than his brutish appearance might lead one to believe, and so he opened the gate and punched in the code without blustering or hesitation, in the hopes that all the pair wanted was to rob the clinic, and not harm anyone.

Sara had her blouse refastened, and she retrieved the van and drove it into the parking lot, and once they were inside the clinic, Duke smashed the gun against the side of J.T.'s head, and the big man fell to the floor, stunned.

Laurel appeared, and ran to the guard's side to help him.

"Oh God, what are you doing?"

"He'll be fine," Duke said, and he flipped the guard over and used zip ties to bind the man's hands behind his back, before placing larger ties around his ankles.

Laurel had been down on the floor beside J.T., checking the cut on his scalp, when Sara pulled her to a standing position and pointed a gun at her.

"I want you to get Tanner here. Call him!"

Laurel looked down at the gun, and then up at Sara.

"Wasn't killing Johnny enough? Does Tanner have to die as well?"

"It's kill or be killed when it comes to Tanner, and I don't intend to die."

After saying this, Sara's expression softened, and she sniffled and took a deep breath.

"I'm so sorry that Johnny had to pay for my mistakes, and I'm sorry that I have to use you too."

"Use me?" Laurel said.

"Yes, you're the bait that will place Tanner in my trap, and if I'm right, he'll snap it shut on himself."

"You want to kill Tanner, but it won't turn out that way, he'll kill you instead."

"You'd better hope not."

"Why?"

"Because if I die, then so do you."

***

Tanner arrived within minutes of receiving Laurel's call, and he came alone.

He and Duke kept their guns pointed at each other as Duke let him inside, and he stepped past the now fully aware, but bound and gagged, J.T.

However, as soon as Tanner spotted Laurel and Sara, all else faded into the background.

Sara was standing with her left forearm locked around Laurel's throat, while with her right hand, she pressed her gun firmly against the side of Laurel's head.

The situation was nearly identical to one Tanner faced days earlier when the assassin Gerda held Sophia hostage.

Tanner had ended that standoff with a well-placed shot to Gerda's throat, and luckily, the woman had not fired in reflex and killed Sophia.

Such an act now seemed not only dangerous to Tanner, but cavalier as well, and he could not imagine risking Laurel's life in a similar fashion.

"I tried not to underestimate you, Blake, and I wound up overestimating you. I really believed that you would keep your word, but you're just a lying little bitch, aren't you?"

"I had every intention of keeping my word, it's just that the situation… I… what does it matter? This is where we are now."

Tanner looked at Laurel, and searched her for signs of abuse.

"Has she hurt you, Laurel?"

"No, but I believe her when she says that she'll kill me."

"Let her go, Blake. This is between you and me."

"No Tanner, this, is between you, me, and Brian Ames, the man you killed, the man I loved."

"The way you loved Rossetti? Johnny is dead because of you, Blake, because you couldn't keep your word and let the past be."

"I know I'm to blame, but it was only because I believed, no, because I knew that you wouldn't keep your word, and that you couldn't be trusted."

"You were wrong. My word is about all I have in this world, and when I say I'm going to do a thing, I do it."

"I see that now, and as amazing as it is to me, I believe that you would have let me live."

"It's too late for that now," Tanner said, and he raised his gun and pointed it at Sara's head.

Duke moved towards him, and the guard, who was seated on the floor with his back against the wall, thrust out his bound feet, and tripped Duke, who stumbled, but kept his balance.

Tanner spun on Duke in an instant, and caught the man across the bridge of his crooked nose with the barrel of his gun, which broke the nose once more, and then he wrenched Duke's gun out of his hand.

Duke cried out in pain from the blow, as he leaned against the wall, while Tanner, after using his knife to free J.T.'s hands, gave the big man Duke's gun.

Sara saw that her plan was falling apart and she issued an ultimatum.

"Stop Tanner, or I swear I'll blow Laurel's brains out."

With the guard keeping an eye on Duke, Tanner walked back over to Sara, and once again pointed his gun at her.

"Let her go. She's an innocent, and I can understand you breaking your word while in the grip of paranoia, but Blake, I don't think that you would kill an innocent."

Sara let out a laugh that teetered on the edge of hysteria.

"She may be an innocent, but she's also karma."

"What the hell are you talking about?"

"An eye for an eye, Tanner, you killed someone that I loved, and now I'll kill someone that you care about. I'll still die, but I'll have a little payback as I go."

Tanner lowered his arm after hearing those words, as a chill ran down his spine.

Laurel spoke as tears fell from her eyes.

"I don't think this is going to work out well for me, is it Tanner?"

Tanner grimaced after hearing the tone of desolation in Laurel's words, and with his left hand, he reached up and brushed her tears away.

"I won't let anything happen to you."

Laurel smiled, opened her mouth, and bit down hard on Sara's forearm.

Sara yelped in pain, but she tightened her grip and then jammed her weapon sideways into Laurel's mouth.

"No!" Tanner screamed, even as he thrust his gun against Sara's head.

"Do you love this woman, Tanner?" Sara asked. "Because if you do, the only way to save her is to give yourself up,"

Tanner pressed his gun into the side of Sara's head as he spoke through gritted teeth.

"Let her go, Blake!"

"The only way that happens is if you surrender. She might live if you pull that trigger, but given where my gun is located, I doubt that outcome."

Tanner looked at Laurel. She was gagging on the gun, and her eyes were filled with the fear of death.

Tanner removed his gun from Sara's head, took a step back, and spoke to Laurel.

"You asked me if I loved you, and I didn't answer… but I'm answering you now."

Tanner's arm lowered, and he let his gun drop to the floor.

Sara sighed with relief, and removed her gun from Laurel's mouth.

"Duke?" Sara said, and Duke held out his hand towards the bodyguard.

"Give him back his gun," Tanner said, and J.T. reluctantly complied.

Sara still held her gun on Laurel, and she kept it there until Duke had Tanner's hands cuffed behind his back. Still, when Laurel moved towards Tanner, Sara held her back with a hand on her arm.

Tanner glared at her.

"Are you going to keep your word and let Laurel live, or are you going to break it like you did last time?"

The question stung Sara, who always thought of herself as a person of honor, and she considered her severing of their truce as an anomaly, one which was spawned by desperation and fear.

She released Laurel and lowered her weapon.

"I won't hurt her, ever."

As Duke was herding Tanner towards the door with a gun pressed against the back of his head, Laurel called to him.

"I love you, Tanner!"

He turned, ignored the gun now pointed at his face, and spoke words that hurt every bit as much as they healed.

"I love you too, Laurel, and I always have."

And then he walked out into the night, a captive not only of love, but of a woman who wanted him dead.

***

Tanner was propped up against the right wall in the rear of Duke's van, with his shackled hands behind his back and chained to a ring in the floor.

His ankles were shackled as well, and a second chain was around his neck and connected to the wall behind him.

Tanner felt not only defeated, but broken.

He had long believed that love was for fools, and he had never counted himself among their ilk. Now, he knew that he was not only one of them, but possibly their king.

He handed himself over to an enemy he knew would kill him, and he did so out of love, while placing another's welfare in front of his own survival.

In his eyes, that made him just another fool, no different than his father, whose love for a woman brought about not only his own destruction, but that of his family as well.

Tanner thought of Laurel, knew that he'd never see her again, and that thought was bitter and more grievous to him than the knowledge that his death was imminent.

***

Sara, her arm bloody from Laurel's bite, sat across from Tanner with a gun pointed his way, and with her long sought victory now a reality. But her triumph was a pyrrhic one, costing her not only her honor, but also the life of Johnny Rossetti, a man she had come to love.

"Tanner?"

He didn't answer her. He saw no point in talking, but she called his name once more and he pulled his gaze from the floor and stared at her.

"What is it, Blake?"

"I won't torture you."

Tanner gazed at her, as a bittersweet smile played at the corners of his mouth.

"You already have,"

The van rolled on, headed towards a place of execution, and Tanner's only hope was that fate somehow showed him mercy. However, like himself, fate was not known to be so inclined.

SUICIDE OR DEATH
A TANNER NOVEL - BOOK 7

A SPECIAL SNEAK PEEK OF

REDEMPTION
BY
REMINGTON KANE

CHAPTER 1

Robbinstown, California, 5:22 a.m.

When he stopped drinking heavily, his sister thought that it was a good sign.

She believed that he was finally working through his depression, and in a way, she was right.

However, Jake Stelton knew that he had passed through his months of depression only to find himself living in total despair.

He had stopped drinking because he no longer needed it to get through his days. It was similar to the way a driver turns off their headlights when they were at last exiting a long, dark tunnel.

Jake was exiting his own dark tunnel, the tunnel of his life.

***

He'd been up all night, wandering the family farm while he thought about his life, debating whether to leave a note and finally deciding against it. He sat on a tree stump, the gun in his right hand, dangling between his legs.

The five-shot revolver held only one bullet, and it wasn't just any gun. It was a Smith & Wesson model 500, one of the most powerful handguns made. It was not enough to put a bullet in his brain; no, Jake wanted to obliterate the treacherous organ.

To his right, laid acres of ripening corn, as to his left, the sun, newly risen, peeked above the hills of his farm, a farm that had been in his family for six generations. The place where he was born; and the place where he will die,

A tumor, a renegade growth of cells, had expanded its useless self until it grew large enough to damage the left, lateral ventricle region of his brain and placed his mind in shambles.

Although the tumor turned out to be benign, its rate of growth was rapid, and changed Jake into a man tortured by paranoid delusions. Delusions that led to him taking Kelly Rodgers hostage, and, which caused him to shoot five innocent people to death.

"Kelly," Jake whispered, as his eyes grew moist and he tightened his grip on the gun.

He and Kelly had only been together for a few months, but they were in love and talking of marriage when signs of the tumor first surfaced.

Now, it made him wince in agony to think how much she feared him. Although medical science and the legal system found him guiltless of blame for his actions, Kelly could not forget what had happened and even refused to talk to him.

"She fears you more than she loves you." Kelly's sister, Kate, had told him, while he lay in his hospital bed recovering from brain surgery. Even now, all these long months later, Jake knew that Kelly didn't go anywhere without a bodyguard; she was still fearful that insanity would once again grip his mind and turn him into a monster.

A monster,

It's what they called him in the papers, while beneath the headlines sat the photos of the five innocents

2

he had killed.

He may have been adjudicated innocent due to the tumor, but the public found him guilty of all charges and now he was little more than a pariah.

Death threats were a daily occurrence during his first few weeks of freedom, but tapered off, only to be replaced by a campaign of escalating vandalism that recently culminated with the death of his sister's beloved horse, Molly.

Someone shot the animal while it wandered in a pasture. The police promised to look into the incident, but were less than sympathetic.

He needed to leave.

For his sister, and for Kelly,

He needed to leave and let them get on with their lives, to let them live without the turmoil he brought to them just by breathing air.

It was time to leave.

Jake nodded to himself, as he bent his arm and aimed the gun at his face.

I'll take your fear away, baby.

He then opened his mouth to receive the gun.

Movement!

To his right, amidst the cornstalks, and then the sound reached him, the sound of a helicopter closing in fast,

Jake looked up and was astonished to find that the chopper was only two hundred feet or so above his head. He spotted the FBI markings on the black craft and realized that it must have stealth capabilities; he also took note of the nest of cameras festooned to the bottom of it.

A moment later, the air filled with the pilot's voice shouting over a loudspeaker.

"SUBJECT IS AT MY SIX O'CLOCK AND IS ARMED. I REPEAT; THE SUBJECT IS HOLDING A WEAPON."

They seemed to come from every direction at once. As four men in suits stepped from the corn, while to his left and in front of him, police officers from town converged on him, badges sparkling on their blue uniforms, their weapons drawn and aimed right at him.

A voice shouted from behind, "Drop the gun now, Stelton!" It was a voice he remembered well. The voice of Special Agent Vince Callahan,

Jake spoke as he dropped the weapon.

"Callahan, what the hell is going on?"

Callahan answered by tackling him to the ground. He then yanked on Jake's right arm, as he began to handcuff him. Once Jake's hands were manacled behind his back, Callahan patted him down, while the rest of the men gathered around in a semi-circle, and the chopper hovered overhead, nearly silent.

Then, Callahan and another FBI agent sat Jake up and leaned his back against the tree stump. One of the other agents slipped on a latex glove and retrieved Jake's gun from where he dropped it, he then gave the barrel a sniff, as he eyed the cylinder.

"I don't think it's been fired recently Vince, but there's only one shell left in it."

"Thanks Mike," Callahan said to the man, next, he glared down at Jake. "Where is she?"

Jake looked up and saw seven hard faces staring

back at him.

"Where is who? Callahan, what the hell is going on?"

"Kelly Rodgers, Stelton, what have you done with her this time?"

"Kelly?" Jake said, and attempted to sit up straight. Callahan pushed him back against the tree stump with a rough shove.

"The courts won't be fooled twice, Stelton. No judge in the world is going to set you free this time, tumor or not. Now tell us where she is and save us the trouble of searching this damn farm of yours for her body."

"Body? What the... someone's taken her? Kelly is missing?"

Callahan gave him a look of hatred. He was a tall man in his late-forties, with dark hair sprinkled with white. A distance runner in his youth, Callahan had maintained his fitness, and his dogged determination had helped to make him an excellent agent. When Jake had been driven mad by the tumor, it was Callahan who risked his life to stop him.

"Where is she, Stelton?"

"I don't know what you're talking about. I haven't seen Kelly in nearly a year. Is she missing? You're saying that someone has her?"

The next instant, Jake grunted in pain as one of the policemen kicked him in the stomach.

"Did you kill her this time?" the man yelled, as Callahan shoved him away from Jake.

Callahan let out a curse, and stuck a finger in the cop's face.

"We're not here to write a speeding ticket, now stay back and let us handle this."

The cop sent Callahan a hard look, but kept his mouth shut.

Callahan turned back to Jake and took him by an elbow, to help him to stand.

"Damn you, Stelton, where is she?"

Jake looked at him, eyes pleading to be believed, as in the back of his mind a clock had begun ticking, a countdown clock that wouldn't wind down until he knew that Kelly was safe.

"I haven't taken her, Callahan. I'm telling you it wasn't me. If she's missing, if someone has her, you've got to find her. Do you hear me? I didn't do anything. You're looking at the wrong man."

Callahan stared back at him, as he sighed and nodded his head in understanding. He then turned and spoke to the agent on his right.

"Bring in the team, cadaver dogs, backhoes, everything, let's tear this place apart."

Jake cursed under his breath.

"I don't have her, Callahan. You're looking in the wrong place damn you, and it might cost Kelly her life. You've got to look elsewhere; I didn't do anything. It's not me!"

Callahan shoved him at the cop that had kicked him.

"Take him."

Another officer joined the cop, and they began walking Jake away.

"Callahan!" Jake shouted uselessly, then the cop

punched him in the stomach, and he and the other cop dragged him away.

CHAPTER 2

Jake was in the barn, sitting on the floor with his back against a post and his hands cuffed behind him.

He hadn't been read his rights, but then, he hadn't seen anyone in hours. Callahan was making him sweat while he and his agents searched the farm.

They were wasting time that Kelly didn't have and it was driving Jake insane.

He had been alone at the farm last night, as his sister, Claire, had gone away overnight with her boyfriend to visit his family.

The timing had decided the date of his suicide, because he didn't want his sister to be the one that would find his body, and he had hoped that he'd be discovered by one of the farm hands and his remains removed before her scheduled return.

Now, Claire would be returning to even more chaos and Kelly's fate was unknown.

He had to find Kelly, but first he had to get free.

The barn door slid open and Callahan walked in with another agent, Agent Mike Martin, a man with stark white hair, a middle-aged face, and a youthful body.

Callahan knelt down in front of Jake and spoke in a calm, deliberate voice.

"It's time to stop denying that you took her and tell us where she is. It's time to tell the truth."

"I already told you the truth. I had nothing to do with Kelly's disappearance."

Callahan reached back over his shoulder and Jake saw the other man hand him something wrapped in a

8

plastic bag. When Callahan held it up by its sealed top, Jake's breathing accelerated and his heart raced.

The object inside the bag was a woman's left shoe, and Jake saw that it was not only covered in dried blood, but also bits of brain tissue.

Jake swallowed hard as he felt his eyes grow moist.

"Is she dead? Is Kelly dead?"

Callahan stood and handed the bag back to the other agent.

"The blood and tissue on that shoe belonged to her bodyguard, as you well know, since you're the one that murdered him."

It wasn't until he took a breath that Jake realized that he had stopped breathing.

"I didn't kill him, Callahan, and I did not harm Kelly."

"Then how did that shoe wind up on your farm?"

"You found that *here*? That's not possible,"

Callahan and his man exchanged glances and then both men stared down at Jake with venom in their eyes.

Jake had seen that look before. They wanted to hurt him; they wanted to inflict agony upon him until he would tell them anything they wished to know. Jake also knew that if they were less honorable men that they would do just that, but these were men of the law and they would follow the rules, despite believing that he could possibly help them save an innocent life.

Jake both admired and abhorred their scruples while knowing that he would never live by them.

Jake Stelton was a man who killed his enemies, and when he found the man who took Kelly, and by God, he would, he would kill that man and see Kelly to safety, or he would die in the attempt.

***

His sister, Claire, came running over, as the cops were hustling him towards their patrol car. They were parked in the dirt, near a shed that sat a hundred feet from the farmhouse. The other cop, the one that hadn't hit him, took his gun out of his holster and pointed it at Claire.

"Stay back ma'am; this is police business."

Claire took one look at the gun and skidded to a halt on the uneven ground. She must have just arrived back, as Jake noticed that her overnight bag was sitting by her car. Claire's long, brown hair hung down her back and was tied into a ponytail. Claire was two years older than her thirty-year-old brother, and the two of them had always been very close.

"Why are you arresting my brother? What the hell is going on?" She looked up. "And why is there a helicopter hovering over our farm?"

Jake yelled to her.

"Someone's taken Kelly and they think it was me."

"What? When? When was she taken?"

The cops wouldn't answer her; they opened a back door on the patrol car, shoved Jake inside, and slammed the door shut.

After the cops got in the car, Claire ran up to it and stared in at Jake.

"I know you didn't hurt her, couldn't hurt her. I'll call Mel and we'll meet you in town."

Mel was Claire's boyfriend. He was a lifelong city dweller who, a year earlier, had bought a small, neighboring farm.

As the cop started the engine, Jake's eyes locked onto his sister's.

"I have to find her."

"Find her?"

"They're not looking for her, Claire. They think it was me and they've stopped looking for her. I can't let anything happen to her; I have to find her."

Jake wasn't sure that she had heard him through the glass, but then he watched, as his sister straightened abruptly. A moment later, she nodded at him, as a pained expression clouded her face. She mouthed the words, "Be careful," as a tear rolled down her cheek.

And then the cop peeled out, leaving Claire standing alone in a cloud of dust.

CHAPTER 3

Lisa Hanes sat waiting, while her boss, managing news editor Gabriel Mendez, perused her notes.

Lisa had dark hair with green eyes and a body that once earned her runner-up status in a local beauty pageant back in her native South Carolina. She'd been living in California ever since going to school at Stanford; but when she spoke, her voice still carried the sound of The South.

They were in her apartment in Encino, both wore robes, hers was a frilly pink one, while the one Gabe wore was also hers, but made of terry cloth. It was also pink.

Gabe looked up.

"This isn't enough for a story."

He had a New York accent and a perpetual look of skepticism.

Lisa got up from the chair she was sitting in and sat beside him on her sofa.

"I know that I don't have hard facts, yet, but don't you find it strange that so many people are standing by his side? I mean, Christ, Gabe, Anne Bishop's own mother believes that he's incapable of having harmed her, so why are the police so certain that he killed her?"

Gabe ran a hand through his mop of dark curly hair.

"Maybe it's because it makes sense? Everyone else in the case has a solid alibi, everyone but her husband Jimmy. He says he went out for a run, and when he came back, she was gone. Really? So then how did her blood get in the trunk of his car?"

"He can't explain that."

Gabe grinned. "The police can,"

"I want you to talk to him. If you talk to him, you'll see that he's telling the truth."

"The guy's probably a sociopath."

"Sociopath? He's one of the most caring, giving men I've ever met. He works for a non-profit and also volunteers at a nursing home."

Gabe sent her a shrug.

"Maybe he snapped,"

"Go talk to him, please? I truly believe he's innocent and if we can find something the cops missed we'll have an exclusive, since everyone else is vilifying him."

"I'll talk to him, but I still say he probably just went nuts and killed her, and oh yeah, speaking of mental cases, your boy Stelton is in trouble again. Someone snatched Kelly Rodgers last night and the cops think it was him."

Lisa stood up and stared down at Gabe.

"Jake is in jail?"

"He will be soon. I got the call while you were in the shower. The Feds are crawling all over his farm; hopefully they'll find her alive."

Lisa shook her head.

"Jake wouldn't hurt her, he loves her."

Gabe chuckled.

"Right, the tumor, listen, I know that the judge fell for that story, but three other doctors testified that a tumor like the one he had wouldn't make you go crazy the way he did."

"They were wrong. It had to be the tumor, Jake's a

good man."

"Tell that to the five people he shot from that rooftop," Gabe said, and watched as Lisa winced, while recalling that day. He stood up and took her in his arms. "I know you and he had a thing over in Afghanistan, but—"

"It's not that. I was a green reporter in a war zone, trying to prove myself, and scared out of my mind. Jake got me through it. He also saved my life over there."

Gabe released her and held her at arm's length, to study her face.

"Do you love him?"

Lisa leaned forward and kissed him on the mouth.

"No, maybe a little at one time, but no, I love you now."

Gabe kissed her back.

"I love you too, baby."

They fell onto the sofa, while wrapped in each other's arms.

"I want the story, Gabe."

"Charlie, the cameraman, he's picking you up in half an hour."

Lisa turned in his arms and kissed him again.

"Thank you."

"Don't thank me; we both know that you would have gone anyway. Just promise me that you'll be careful. I've read Jake Stelton's file, and tumor or no tumor, he's one dangerous man."

CHAPTER 4

Jake, his hands shackled behind him, sat leaning against the door, as the patrol car slowed near the entrance to his farm. There were two other cops there, and a barricade blocked the exit to the county road.

One of the cops, the one that had hit him, got out of the car and approached the other officers.

"Feds want us to take him in and lock him up."

One of the new cops nodded his head.

"Sergeant Stevens says you're to hold him there until the Feds or the Staties show up. It'll probably be the Feds; the State Police have got their hands full with that tractor-trailer pileup over on the interstate. They say there were three fatalities and a toxic waste spill, it sounds like a mess."

"So what are we supposed to do, baby-sit him all day?"

"Shit runs downhill, Bob, you know that."

The cop, the one named Bob, the one that had hit him, got back into the car with the other cop, the one with the long hair, the one that had pointed his weapon at his sister. When they drove away from the farm, Jake was relieved to see that the other cops stayed behind to man the barricades.

Handcuffed and unarmed against two cops he had a chance, against four, not much chance at all.

"Why only five?" said the cop that hit him,

"What?" Jake said.

"You had a bullet left in the cylinder, that means

15

you must have shot her five times, but why only five?"

"He was gonna off himself, you know, murder/suicide, and he must have shot her four times, a gun like that only holds five because the bullets are so big." said the other cop, long hair, and now Jake detected a faint scent of alcohol on the man's breath.

"Where's she at?" asked the first cop, "Did you dump her somewhere, or is the body buried on your farm?"

Jake stared at the man, and as he realized he had an opening, he smirked.

"Why would I tell a jerkwater cop like you anything? I'll wait and confess to the real cops, the Feds."

"Watch your mouth, and screw the Feds."

Jake gave a little chuckle.

"You shouldn't speak about your betters that way, Deputy Fife, if someone hears you, maybe they'll have you busted to school crossing guard, or would that be a promotion?"

The cop turned beet red and Jake was sure he had him, but a moment later, the cop faced forward and just stared out the window.

Jake cursed inwardly, infuriating the cop wasn't going to work.

Just as he was considering kicking out the side window, the cop shouted to his partner.

"Travis, take the road to the old Miller place, I'm gonna show this prick who *his* betters are."

"Bob, the sergeant will have our balls if—"

"Make the damn turn, Travis!"

The other cop cursed, and a few moments later, he

made a right onto a dirt road. They were going to the Miller place. Jake knew it well, he had played there as a kid, right up until the time that Ronny Miller's parents divorced and Ronny had moved off to San Diego with his mom, and her new boyfriend.

They parked the patrol car near the front steps of the house. The house was a dilapidated shell; two months after Ronny Miller moved away, lightning hit a tree near the house one night, and by morning, the two-story colonial was a burnt hulk. It had been sitting neglected ever since.

The cop named Bob jumped out of the car and ripped open the back door; he reached in, grabbed a fistful of Jake's hair and yanked him off the backseat.

Jake went sprawling onto the grass, thumping hard onto his backside, where he stayed, waiting, knowing that the cop wasn't done yet, and needing him to get closer if his plan was going to work.

The cop took out his nightstick and gave Jake a thump on his left leg. The blow hurt Jake, but he gritted his teeth and smiled up at the cop.

"That's all you got Bobby boy? Hell, my sister hits harder than that."

The cops eyes went wide and he gripped the nightstick with both hands; he then raised it up high, preparing to bring it crashing down upon Jake's skull. Jake flipped his body into a sudden, violent roll and knocked the cop's feet out from under him. The cop fell backwards and Jake rolled again, this time, on top of the man. Jake headbutted the cop on the nose and then he and the cop struggled on the ground a bit until the other cop came over and shoved Jake aside.

The cop got up from the ground covered in dirt and with his uniform shirt ripped open, as blood began dripping from his nose. He glared down at Jake.

"You son of a bitch, you made my nose bleed."

"It serves you right, Bob," Longhair said. "Now how the hell are we going to explain your bloody shirt to the Sergeant?"

"I'll just say he attacked me as we were taking him out of the car, that's all."

Longhair shook his head.

"That won't work, there will probably be other people around when we get there, maybe even reporters, and they're going to see that your shirt is already bloody. Damn it Bob! You just got me in a whole shitload of trouble for nothing."

"I got you in a shitload of trouble? Who do you think has been covering for you the last few months, Travis? Hell, if it wasn't for me, the sarge would have found out what a drunk you are years ago."

"I'm not a drunk! I just drink a little too much sometimes, that's all."

Sitting on the ground behind them, Jake worked feverishly on getting the cuffs off.

While holding the cop's badge in his right hand, he maneuvered the head of the badge's pin into the keyhole of the cuff on his left wrist. At last, he hit the correct spot and the cuff sprang open.

The cop with the bloody nose walked over and stood in front of him, while glaring down in hatred. He then took his gun out and pointed it at Jake's face.

"In for a penny, in for a pound, I'm already in trouble, so I've got nothing to lose. You're gonna tell us what you did with Kelly Rodgers and you're gonna tell us now, otherwise, I'm gonna beat the living shit out of you."

"I can't tell you what I don't know," Jake said.

The cop turned the gun around in his hand, so that now he was holding it by the barrel, like a club. Before he could raise it up to strike, Jake reached out and wrest it from his hand. He then stood and jammed the gun into the cop's belly.

"You!" Jake shouted to the other cop. "Take out your weapon and throw it away or I'll shoot your partner. Try and shoot me and I'll use him as a shield, and then I'll blast right through him to hit you."

The cop just stood there frozen for a moment, with his hand halfway to his holster. Then, with a whispered curse, he unsnapped his holster and slowly removed his weapon in a two-fingered grip.

While he was doing that, Jake was busy holding the other cop up with his free hand, as the man's knees had given up on him. After the cop with the long hair tossed his gun aside, Jake stepped back and let the first cop sink to the ground; in the man's eyes was a haunted look of fear.

"Don't kill me, mister, don't kill me," the cop pleaded.

Jake held out his left hand.

"Toss me your keys."

The cop fumbled in his side pocket for a few seconds and produced a ring of keys; he flipped them to Jake, and Jake used them to unlock the last cuff.

"Take off your radios and empty your pockets... wallets, cell phones, everything."

They did as they were told and piled it all on the ground. Afterwards, Jake herded them over to a tree and handcuffed them around it, so that the cops looked as if they were hugging opposite sides of the tree.

After grabbing their keys, guns and nightsticks, Jake stared at them.

"I'm not going to hurt you and I didn't abduct Kelly. You'll be fine here. Eventually, someone will find you and by then I'll be long gone."

And with that, Jake turned on his heels and headed for the patrol car. As he placed the car in gear, he looked in the rearview mirror and watched as the cop with the long hair banged the side of his head against the tree. Jake would have taken the action as an act of frustration, and yet, something about the way the cop was doing it seemed purposeful, even methodical.

He shifted the car back into park and got out. Now he could hear the cop talking, giving their location away to someone.

He looked at the pile of the cops' belongings and saw two cell phones lying there alongside their wallets and police radios, and began to wonder if the cop had a second cell phone.

He walked over and studied the man, finding his hands empty, then, reaching up, he brushed back the long hair.

Fitted onto the cop's ear was a Bluetooth device, its little blue light flashing away. He hadn't been banging his head in frustration; he had been activating the

Bluetooth.

Jake yanked the thing off the cop's ear and crushed it with his heel.

"You're too late, Stelton. They know where you are and they're sending the chopper. You might as well give up right now."

Jake punched the man on the side of his chin and watched him sag against the tree.

"That was for pulling your gun on my sister."

Afterwards he smiled at the man, as an idea struck him. Soon after that, he was driving away as fast as he dared.

CHAPTER 5

Claire stood outside by the barn talking to Mel Brady, her boyfriend and owner of the neighboring farm.

Claire's farm was overrun by federal agents, and Claire was warned to stay out of the farmhouse while they conducted their search. From the sounds of the rummaging and ransacking, Claire thought that their search seemed more like a pillaging than a hunt for clues to Kelly's whereabouts.

Right before she was ushered from her home, she watched as two agents flipped over her new sofa and began cutting the lining from the back of it.

Mel was six-foot-three, well educated and affable to a fault, usually; the only thing that raised his hackles was when someone called him baby face, due to his lineless skin, rosy cheeks and bright blue eyes. A city slicker, he had spent his life as a successful lawyer, specializing in contract law. However, he often reminisced about the summers he had spent as a boy on a favorite uncle's farm.

After a messy divorce, he decided to change his life and buy the farmland bordering Jake and Claire's property; a piece of land that at one time had been a section of the Stelton farm.

Despite the fact that Mel was eleven years older than Claire, the two were immediately attracted to each other. Mel saw her through the chaos of Jake's earlier… troubles, and he listened to her now as she relayed to him what Jake told her.

"What did he mean by, 'He's got to find her'? He'll be in jail soon; he won't be able to look for her."

"He's going to escape."

"But how, Claire? You said he was taken away in handcuffs."

Before Claire could answer, the sight of several agents dashing to their vehicles and speeding away startled her. Special Agent Vince Callahan rushed over with a female agent and introduced her to Claire.

"Ms. Stelton, this is Agent Sandra Randolph, Agent Randolph will be your escort until further notice."

"What's happened? Is my brother all right?"

"No ma'am, your brother is far from all right, not only has he abducted Kelly Rodgers again but now he's also assaulted the two police officers assigned to take him to jail."

Claire grinned. "He's escaped?"

"Yes, but I wouldn't be so pleased about it if I were you. We'll soon have him back in custody and this attempted escape will only make things worse for him."

"He's not trying to run away, Agent Callahan; He's doing the job that you should be doing; he's going to find Kelly. My brother didn't take her. He would never hurt her."

Callahan stared at Claire with a look that was equal parts anger and pity.

"Ms. Rodgers was being protected by a bodyguard when she was abducted. Someone came up from behind and blew his brains out, forensics place the shooter at less than a foot away. Do you know anyone capable of killing someone in cold blood, hmm?"

"Yes, my brother is capable of killing, but he killed for his country, in the line of duty. He didn't take Kelly."

"I know five people that would disagree, except they're all dead, and it was your brother that murdered them."

"He was sick, goddamn you! He was sick and he didn't know what he was doing."

"That's what the court said too; only you and the court didn't have to face those people's families after your brother walked off scot-free, I did."

Claire stared down at the ground.

"Jake would never hurt Kelly; he loves her."

Callahan's voice softened as he placed a hand on her shoulder.

"We've found one of Ms. Rodgers' shoes on your farm. It was bloody, preliminary tests say that the blood type matches the bodyguard that was killed. Your brother is dangerous. Maybe he's lost his mind or maybe not, but either way he's our best hope of locating Kelly Rodgers and I won't stop until I find her."

"You found Kelly's shoe here?"

Callahan nodded.

Claire's mouth opened in shock.

"Oh my God, someone's framing Jake."

This time, the look Callahan offered her was pure pity.

The helicopter appeared overhead and Callahan pointed towards a nearby field. He told Claire, "Stay with Agent Randolph," and jogged out to the field and climbed aboard the chopper.

Agent Randolph stood before Claire with a look that said she'd brook no nonsense. She was a tall woman with short dark hair and ice-blue eyes.

"Please come with me into the house, ma'am."

Claire nodded to her and then spoke to Mel.

"Can you stay?"

"Not right now; but I'll be back later."

"All right, I love you."

"I love you too, Claire."

Claire turned and began walking toward the house, but then she swiveled about.

"Mel!"

"Yeah?"

"Jake didn't do this."

"How can you be sure?"

She hesitated a moment before answering.

"My brother is a lot of things, clever among them, but he's not devious. If he wanted Kelly dead, she'd be dead and there would be no doubt about who did it."

Mel sent her a nod and then watched her go into the house with Agent Randolph. A moment later, he turned and bolted towards his home like a man on a mission.

***

Jake made a fishtailing left turn back onto the dirt road as he exited the Miller place in the stolen police car, and made another hard left back onto the county road.

Afterwards, he lowered the windows and tried to listen for the sound of approaching sirens over the whoosh of the traffic, as he sped the car along.

Up ahead on the right, a dirt road appeared, it was actually not much more than a wide trail and Jake made a sharp turn onto it. A few hundred yards along, he parked the patrol car under a stand of shady trees.

After hitting the trunk release, he jumped out of the car and listened intently, knowing that the chopper would be searching the area for the police car, which sported a huge black 8 atop its white roof.

He saw the chopper before he heard it. The near-silent craft was hovering over the roadway, back near the Miller place. Behind him, out on the road, a caravan of black cars appeared, and as the lead car slowed, he knew that the patrol car had been spotted.

After putting the car in drive, he aimed it at a vast acreage of strawberry plants that stretched to the horizon. With the chopper in pursuit, the car bounced its way across the plants, sending up a plume of cloaking dust as it raced for freedom.

***

Inside the chopper, Callahan instructed the pilot to follow the car and then used his headset to speak to the third man in the craft, a man who was holding a rifle with a scope.

"What do you think, Simmons, can you shoot out the tires?"

"I could try, but look at that car. The way he's bouncing along in that thing I'd doubt he'd even notice, he must be doing sixty down there."

"Sixty-three and climbing," The pilot corrected.

Callahan shook his head.

"Where the hell is he headed? Where's this damn field end?"

"Up ahead is the freeway, and oh yeah, a truck stop," the pilot said.

"That's where he's headed, the truck stop. He's

probably planning on hitching a ride with a departing truck. Simmons, forget the tires; I need you to disable that damn car now."

"Get me in front of it and I'll take out the engine."

The pilot flew ahead of the car until he was only a hundred yards from a grassy slope that led up to the interstate. He then hovered twenty feet off the ground, while the marksman, Simmons, lined up the car in his sights.

Simmons had a frustrated expression showing as he looked through the riflescope.

"Damn it, he's throwing up so much dust that I can barely see the car."

Callahan placed a hand on his shoulder.

"You can do it. Take out that engine, but don't put any rounds into the passenger compartment. We need Stelton alive; we have to know what he did with Kelly Rodgers."

"Right," Simmons said, then, after taking a deep breath, he fired repeatedly into the engine compartment of the patrol car, on a downward angle.

At first, it appeared as if the shots had no effect, but then the car lurched violently, as if the brakes were being stomped. Seconds later, the car drifted toward the left as it slowed, and soon, it came to a sputtering, steam-filled stop.

A few moments later, the first of the pursuing vehicles caught up to the car, and within seconds, there were six FBI agents out of their vehicles with weapons drawn.

As soon as the chopper landed, Callahan jump to

the ground and joined his men. He then spoke to a man with premature white hair and gray eyes.

"What did the cops have to say, Mike?"

"Jacobs is headed there now with one of the other town cops; Stelton left them somewhere called the Miller place. I told him to take them back to town and that we would debrief them when this is over."

"You sent Jacobs? That kid is as green as they come."

"Not as green as we were."

Callahan grinned. "Ain't that the truth,"

Callahan was handed a pair of binoculars and sighted in on the car,

"That car is a wreck after racing through these fields; if we hadn't shot up the motor I bet the suspension would have given out."

"We were following him at half his speed and I felt like I was in a clothes dryer. I could barely keep my hands on the wheel as bumpy as it was."

Callahan squinted through the binoculars. The damn thing is so covered with dust that I can't see through the windows."

"Yeah," Mike said. "It hasn't rained here for a while and it's been hot for days now, but he's still hunkered down in there, I saw movement when we pulled up."

"All right, if we have to, we'll wait him out. The cop that made the call said that Stelton took their weapons, so we know that he's armed."

"Yeah, but Kelly Rodgers could be running out of time if we don't make him talk soon. Do you think he's killed her?"

Callahan sighed.

"I don't know what to think when it comes to Stelton. What I do know is that he's a better shot than anyone here will ever be, and because of that, we have to tread carefully. Hand me that loud-hailer, will you?"

Martin handed Callahan the loud-hailer and he turned it on and spoke.

"JAKE STELTON, THIS IS SPECIAL AGENT CALLAHAN. STEP OUT OF THE VEHICLE WITH BOTH HANDS IN THE AIR, NOW!"

No answer, but the car started a violent rocking.

"What the hell is he doing in there, having a fit?"

"Your guess is as good as mine, Mike."

Mike's phone rang and he looked at the caller ID.

"It's Jacobs,"

Martin answered the call, listened, and then cursed.

"What is it?"

"Jacobs says that Stelton took one of the cops with him as a hostage."

"Well that changes things, but not everything. We've still got him cornered and hostage or no hostage, he's not getting away."

Callahan raised the loud-hailer again.

"STELTON, WE KNOW YOU HAVE A HOSTAGE. TELL US WHAT YOU WANT."

No answer, but again, the car rocked violently up and down.

Martin cocked his head.

"What the hell is he doing in there?"

Callahan nibbled at his bottom lip.

"I don't know, plus it's getting hot and he's keeping the windows shut tight so that we can't see him. The forecast calls for high eighties today; he'll soon be a sweaty mess and dying for a drink of water, if worse comes to worst, I guess we'll just wait him out."

The car rocked again, and this time, a voice carried in the wind.

"Did you hear that, Vince?"

Callahan nodded. He continued staring at the car and watched as it rocked again. He then hung his head when he realized what had happened.

"Mike, do you still have that body shield in your car?"

"Yeah, but I thought we were going to wait him out, soften him up a little?"

"I got a bad feeling, and a hunch, go get the shield."

Mike came back with the shield. It was a four-foot high piece of curved material composed of a black, bullet-resistant fiber; at the top was a clear, polycarbonate lens to see through, and at the back, a horizontal handle.

Callahan talked into the loud-hailer.

"STELTON, I'M COMING OVER TO TALK AND I'M COMING ALONE."

Martin grabbed his arm.

"Alone? Vince, that's not a good idea; let me back you up?"

"If my hunch is right, I'm in no danger."

Martin gave his boss a quizzical look and watched as he eased towards the police car with the shield held in front of him.

Callahan walked to within five feet of the trunk and called out.

"Stelton, lower the window and let's talk."

The car rocked more violently than before and Callahan could hear muffled cries emanating from the trunk. He moved slowly along the driver's side and strained to look through the dust-covered windows. No good, the few sections of glass that weren't covered by dust were stained red from the thousands of strawberries that the car had mown down.

Callahan stood before the driver's door. After holstering his weapon, he stretched a tentative hand around the edge of the shield and snatched the door open.

Empty.

On the passenger seat laid one of the stolen guns along with a nightstick and an open Print Kit, the kind of kit the police used to gather fingerprint evidence. Callahan looked down at the gas pedal, and saw that Jake had taped one end of a nightstick onto the pedal by using the frosted latent print tape from the kit; the other end was jammed through a hole cut in the seat's upholstery.

Callahan reached down and hit the trunk release. The instant after the trunk's lid popped open, officer Travis Connors of the Robbinstown Police Department dropped to the ground with a look of relief in his wild eyes. He was sweaty, gagged and handcuffed. He also suffered from multiple cuts and bruises acquired from his rough ride in the trunk.

Callahan left him as he was and rushed back over to Martin.

"We've got ourselves a manhunt!"

TO CONTACT:

<www.remingtonkane.com>

tannerseries@gmail.com

A PLEA

Thank you, precious reader, for spending time with Tanner. I hope you enjoyed the book. If you did, please consider writing a review. Without reviews, an author's books are virtually invisible on the retail sites. Let other readers know what you thought! You can leave a review by visiting the book's page, and I will greatly appreciate it.

Thank you!

—Remington Kane

ALSO BY REMINGTON KANE

INEVITABLE I - A TANNER NOVEL - BOOK 1

Hired killer Tanner escapes from a Mexican prison and goes in search of revenge against the man who was to be his latest target.

Mobster Albert Rossetti thought he was safe after he framed Tanner for drug possession and had him locked away inside a Mexican prison--but Tanner broke out.

Rossetti's made peace with the man who hired Tanner to kill him, and the contract was cancelled, but that means nothing to Tanner, who lives by his own rules.

Tanner is coming for Rossetti, despite the man's hit squad, or the determined and troubled female FBI agent chasing him.

Tanner is coming, Tanner is deadly, and Tanner never fails.

Tanner Returns and The Conglomerate wants him dead.

With their resources and vast troops of lethal thugs, The Conglomerate assumed that killing one man would be easy.

They were wrong!

While Tanner is just one man, he is the last man you want to go to war with, and when he teams up with another target of The Conglomerate, he doubles his chances at surviving.

But this is war, and The Conglomerate plays to win.

Enter Lars Gruber, possibly the greatest assassin in the world, and now he's set his sights on Tanner.

It's hit man vs. hit man and only one can survive.

Tanner's war with The Conglomerate heats up, but also grows more complicated as he becomes embroiled in a power struggle within the Calvino Crime Family.

Sophia Verona, daughter of slain mobster Jackie Verona is in the middle of the conflict, and only Tanner can save her, but first, he has to keep himself alive.

Meanwhile, Conglomerate boss Frank Richards has plans to gain more power, while his former assistant Al Trent grows closer to learning the truth about Tanner's "Death."

Can Tanner survive and start a new life, or will fate snatch away victory at the last instant?

While a storm rages, Tanner faces off with Sara Blake in the small town of Ridge Creek, and neither one will quit until the other is dead.

<u>THE LIFE & DEATH OF CODY PARKER – A TANNER</u>
<u>NOVEL – BOOK 5</u>

In the town of Stark, Texas, Tanner faces ghosts from his past, as he tries to keep history from repeating itself.

ALSO

THE TAKEN! SERIES

Made in the USA
Lexington, KY
20 April 2017